Raven's Climb
Tiffany Casper

Dogwood Treasure

Wrath MC

Book 3

Copyright © Tiffany Casper 2021

All rights reserved. No part of this publication may be reproduced, distributed, or transmitted in any form or by any means, including photocopying, recording, or other electronic or mechanical methods, without the prior written permission of the publisher, except in the case of brief quotations embodied in critical reviews and certain other noncommercial uses permitted by copyright law.

Acknowledgments

Cover Design: Tiffany Casper

Editor: Tammy Carney

Thank you to my team, Cathy, Billie, Shelby, Stracey, and Lindsay!!!

Also thank you to my girls, Collete, Kage, Gretchen, Lin, and Angela!!!

Playlist

I Don't Deserve You – Plumb

That Summer – Garth Brooks

Let It Go – Demi Lovato

Kickin' It In Tennessee – Big SMO

Maggie May – Rod Stewart

Wonderwall – Oasis

In Case You Didn't Know – Brett Young

When A Man Loves A Woman – Percy Sledge

Wrath MC

Dogwood Chapter

Powers – President

Cam – Vice President

Clutch – Tattoo Artist

Heathen – Enforcer

Gage – Sgt. At Arms

Greek – Tech

Zeke – Secretary

Lincoln – Treasurer

Savage – Road Captain

Skinner – Icer

Table Of Contents

Prequel

Prologue

Chapter 1

Chapter 2

Chapter 3

Chapter 4

Chapter 5

Chapter 6

Chapter 7

Chapter 8

Chapter 9

Chapter 10

Chapter 11

Chapter 12

Chapter 13

Chapter 14

Chapter 15

Chapter 16

Chapter 17

Epilogue

Connect With Me

Other Works

Prequel

Wrath MC

The most notorious, dangerous, one-percenter motorcycle club isn't the one everyone knows about. It isn't the one everyone sees at rallies, charity events, or even at bars. Some say Wrath MC is just a myth. A club that was savage, a club that passed around women then sold them to the highest bidder. Others say the MC is full of nine to fivers and weekend warriors. They also say, no one wanted to cross them. Well, some of those myths just may be true. While there are rumors about the club and those are galore, the rumor of where the mother charter could possibly be located is the largest one of all.

The people in a little old county in Tennessee know better. The three hundred square miles in Clearwater held a secret. A very well-known secret or two. Little did they know, Wrath MC holds many more secrets, a lot of those are made of stories your momma warned you about.

Some people have even been rumored to have gone missing in the area, never to be heard from again.

While others have either passed through and are but a fading memory, some have come and gone and left their mark. While others have come and made their mark on not only the MC but on the community as well.

This story is about one of the members of Wrath MC—the Vice President, to be exact.

Hold on for one wild alpha badass man and a romance that will last till the end of time.

Your life can't fall apart if you never had it together.

Prologue

Michelle

Laying in the back of his blanket-covered Chevy S-10 pickup truck underneath the stars on a summer night was magical.

We did things like this often. Sure I was only sixteen and he was seventeen but I knew that he was the man that I was going to spend the rest of my life with. No this wasn't some teenage crush. This was an I see myself spending the rest of my life with this man kind of thing.

Smiling up at Cam, I snuggled closer into his chest, loving the feel of his arms wrapped around me. They say home is where the heart is, I knew in that instance that I was home.

I'd been in love with Cam since I could remember. He was turning eighteen tomorrow and I wanted to give him his birthday present now, but I didn't want to spoil it. I had been wracking my brain all month, thinking of the perfect gift, and one sunny day last week, I had stumbled upon it.

It was a signed paperback of his favorite author, and his favorite book, *Stephen King's The Shining*. I had watched that movie and even though I knew that it was all fake, it scared the bejesus out of me. Who knew that redrum spelled murder?

I sure as heck didn't, God forbid if there was an alcoholic drink on the market with that for its name.

That night after Cam drove me home, he placed a kiss on my temple and said, "Good night beautiful." I melted a little more inside every time he said those words. To be honest I didn't know how much deeper into my heart he could get, turns out, one single action was going to change the rest of my life.

The next day I did my hair in curls because that was what he liked. I had put on a new white cotton sundress that I adored when I had seen it while I had been shopping with my aunt, my father's sister Mae.

Mae didn't live in Tennessee, she had come down on her weekend visit once a month to hang out with me and supposedly give my mother a break, I didn't know why? I really was a good kid. I made all A's in school. I didn't go out and party, why would you need to go out when you could hang out at the clubhouse and get the best of both worlds.

Party and safety. Only what I wouldn't know is that the safety I had felt all my life within this MC was going to be ripped away in the blink of an eye.

An hour later I walked into the clubhouse with Cam's gift, smiling when I saw him. My God, he was gorgeous. I knew that the older he became, the more handsome he would be.

Only he wasn't alone. Mina was on his lap. I froze as I stared at him. I hated Mina with a passion. She was five years older than my sixteen and she was the devil reincarnated. Literally.

Do you want to know how I discovered that holding an ice pack for five to fifteen minutes on a piece of gum got it out of your hair? Mina. It was supposedly an accident that the gum flew out of her mouth because she supposedly tripped. She was a freaking cow.

She never let a moment go to try and embarrass me no matter what it was. Cam knew that I hated Mina. Why just two weeks ago she told the entire clubhouse that I was known around town as a get on my knees kind of girl. She was spreading the rumor about me when it was really about her. Anyone with a pair of eyes would know that. She was a floozy.

Even though I have come to the clubhouse multiple times, walking in here without my mom or Cam was a little different.

You see, my dad had been a member of Wrath MC until pancreatic cancer had taken him from our lives. Three years later it still wasn't easy to breathe when I walked through those big oak doors at the clubhouse.

Taking a deep breath I walked over to where he was sitting, unsure of what was even happening here. "Cam, hey."

In a tone that I had only ever heard him speak in when he was talking to someone he didn't like, he said, "What are you doing here?"

"Umm, it's your birthday." What in the world was going on?

"Yeah well, since it's my birthday I don't want you here. In fact, I don't ever want to see your face again. Time for you to leave."

I noticed everyone in the clubhouse had stopped what they were doing to watch what was happening. It felt as though I were being punked, "What are you talking about?"

"Didn't stutter Michelle, turn on your cheating ass and walk the fuck out of this clubhouse. Do not come back."

I stood there frozen, cheating, what the heck? "Cheating? Cam, I have no idea what you're talking about?"

"Never would have imagined that you would have hurt me like this." I was dumbfounded.

I honestly had no clue what was going on. What had changed between the time I texted him good night when I had gotten in bed until now.

"Son, think you need to take this somewhere private," Powers growled at him.

"Negative Pres. No need to make this private. I was patched in as a brother this morning." He turned his attention back to me, "Mina told me all about it. Saw you with Porter."

I stared at him, lost for words, "Porter? He's our friend. What are you even talking about?"

He stood knocking Mina to the ground as he sneered then pulled out his phone. I would have laughed at the expression on her face however, I was frozen on the spot.

It was then that he pulled out his phone, did something on it, and then shoved the phone in my face.

Jerking my head back in reflex, I squinted my eyes to get a better look.

I stared at some woman with Porter. "What am I looking at?"

He snarled at me; he had never done that to me. "You're fucking joking right?" The sarcasm in his tone was biting.

"No, I'm not Cam. I have no clue what you're even talking about. Why does it matter that Porter is with someone?"

"Oh don't be stupid honey, know your smart, but come the fuck on. I'm not fucking stupid, that someone is you. And you lost the right to call me Cam. It's Cameron to you. Get out of my sight."

"Cam, that isn't me, look at her ears." I pleaded with him. Seeing Mina's smug expression out of the corner of my eye had me wanting to claw her eyes out.

"I've looked at the picture so much I'm sick to my stomach. I'm sick of looking at it and you." I didn't know how much that the next words to come out of his mouth would tear my heart to shreds.

"You're nothing but a piece of trash and a whore." He turned on his booted heel and walked away from me as he headed to the bar.

Never in my wildest dreams would I have imagined the words that would have come out of his mouth. I stared at him, open-mouthed.

Had I really just heard him say that to me? "What are you still doing here? Leave bitch. Get fucking gone." He roared at me.

Through bleary eyes, uncaring that I dropped his gift to the wooden floor as I ran out of the clubhouse.

Through bleary eyes, I hadn't seen the shadow that was leaned up against the building. It wasn't until the shadow fell over me that I realized I had messed up.

A hand had wrapped around my throat and squeezed, stalling the scream that I had tried to let out.

"Be a good little girl for me." And that was the last thing I remembered. Maybe I was just trash as Cam had called me.

***

Cam

Watching her as she turned on her heels and ran away from me, her words had started on a loop, *look at the girl's ears*, she had told me. Snarling as Mina tried to climb in my lap again, I stood and paid no mind when her ass missed my legs and the chair, then she fell to the floor. Again.

I walked up the staircase to my bedroom, closing the door, I leaned my back against it as I tried to take calming breaths. Michelle was my heart. I loved that girl with a fierceness that surprised even me.

I suddenly found my phone in my hand and the picture pulled up. Then I looked at the girl's ears and froze. She had piercings. Michelle didn't have any. In fact upon closer inspection, the girl had a butterfly tattoo at the base of her neck, how the fuck had I missed that?

A cold sweat came over me as I realized what I had just done.

Growling, I turned on my heel, threw open the door, and ran down the stairs of the clubhouse, through the main door, and out to the parking lot.

My eyes scanned the area, looking for her car. Seeing that, I inhaled a breath.

I still had time to make this right. Please let me make this right.

Walking over to her car, I started to run my apology through my mind.

However, everything that was running through my brain was halted.

Everything stopped.

Michelle was lying beside her car with her panties around her feet. Curled up in a protective ball, not moving.

I hadn't realized that I had screamed. Hadn't realized that paramedics were trying to take her from me. Hadn't realized that my brothers had to hold me, to keep me from climbing in the ambulance with her.

Walking to Greek's office I clenched and unclenched my fists. I knocked on the door with my knuckles.

Seeing Greek, his face tightened as he started the feed of the parking lot outside of the compound.

I bit my tongue so hard I tasted blood.

Seeing the man's face smile as Michelle screamed out "No," "Stop," had me wanting to pummel his face in with my bare hands.

An hour later I was at the clubhouse. Placing my clothes in a black trash bag that Heathen had waiting on outside of my room, then I showered.

And that was when the man's face registered in my mind on who the man was that raped Michelle. Fucking Porter. What the actual fuck?

"Get him?" I knew that Greek had ran a facial software program that he had designed, Greek was a fucking genius. Literally. I knew of three government agencies that had tried to recruit him. He had turned them down hard.

I grabbed the piece of paper that had a couple of addresses on it and I hit the road.

I was taking care of this scum before I went to Michelle. Only had I known that I should've waited and gotten to the hospital as fast as I could get there, I would've.

It took me an hour to find the piece of shit.

Bringing my boot up I kicked in the door to Porter's apartment.

Seeing him with his face scratched up wasn't good enough. I didn't give him a minute to say a word as I launched myself at him and hit him with one solid left hook. Seeing him drop to the floor again wasn't good enough.

"Why?" I roared.

"Because you asshole. Our parents left everything to you." He said as he got up on his hands and knees.

"What the fuck are you talking about?" I asked him when he stood back up.

"Ha. Dear old parents never told you? Mom had an affair with my father. We are half-brothers. You got the money they left you and you got the woman that I wanted. Well guess what brother dearest, you got the money but I finally got the woman. Took the one thing that you wanted."

Everything he had to say sounded like acid. "You're fucked up in the head asshole. And you may have taken something from me, but I'll be there to repair the damage you did."

Two hours and the motherfucker took his last breath.

After I dealt with the asshole, having made my first kill at the age of eighteen didn't seem to bother me as it should have. No, the man had hurt mine. Someone I loved deeply, someone who had loved me unconditionally, until I fucked it all up.

Driving to the hospital I vowed that no one would take me from her bedside. No-fucking-one.

The moment I parked outside, I made my way in through the glass doors of the emergency room, walking to the nurse's station, I asked the first nurse I saw, "What room is Michelle O'Connell in?"

I was sure I looked like a mad man; adrenaline was still pumping through my veins.

"And you are?" she sneered as she looked at my kutte that I had gotten this morning.

"Her boyfriend." I all but snarled out. She was wasting my time.

She typed something on her computer, then she floored me when she said, "She was discharged thirty minutes ago."

Running out of the hospital to my bike, I gunned the engine and rode hard for her house.

Only it was her mother that was wiping a tear out of her eyes as she opened the door, glaring at me.

"She isn't here. Nor is she ever coming back." Then with those words, she slammed the door in my face.

Not going to the hospital with her was the one decision that I would regret for the rest of my life.

Walking back into the clubhouse, all of the brothers gave me a wide berth, but it was Melia, the only one to approach me as she held out the gift bag that had been in Michelle's hands.

Tagging it from her, I carried it with care up to my room.

Pulling out my favorite book and seeing that it was signed, my fucking God I had fucked up. Not small. Oh no. Fucking huge.

See, the problem is that God gives men a brain and a penis, and only enough blood to run one at a time.

Chapter 1

Cam

Seven Years Later

"Cam, let's fucking go already," I growled at Gage as I applied oil to my beard. He has been pounding on my door at the clubhouse for the past hour, okay, it was more like five minutes but Jesus Christ.

There was no damn respect in this club. Well not for Gage anyway, fucker didn't care that I was the V.P and he was the SAA.

No, all the fucker cared about was getting laid.

We were all headed out to a new strip club that we had opened up, well all of us except for Powers, Heathen, and Skinner. Powers and Heathen had ole' ladies at home and they didn't care to look at naked women. As for why Skinner wouldn't be coming tonight, that was a story for another time.

It was wrong to feel sorry for another man but I did for Skinner. Fucker had received a horrible blow years ago. Shit that changed everything about him. Gone was the carefree jokester. And in its place was a man that nine times out of ten wore a hood over his head. A man that never spoke but one word and that was fucking rare.

When people met Heathen he at least would say a few words, but Skinner, yeah that wasn't going to happen.

The reason why Greek was going tonight was that Melia was going. When she had heard our plans for the evening she had given Greek a look. The man looked thrilled, to say the least.

No way I could ever be in a relationship like theirs. Sure they had been together for going on years, and they felt the need to spice things up but no way in fucking hell would I allow another man to touch what was mine. And no way in hell would I expect my woman to allow another woman's hands on me.

Fuck that shit.

"Keep your fucking pantyhose on," I growled out at him.

As soon as I finished I stomped to the door and threw it open. "What's the fucking rush?"

"We don't hurry up; we won't have a good seat to see the women up on the stage." He grumbled.

"Brother, we own the motherfucker. We have a reserved section for a fucking reason." I reminded him.

"Oh yeah. Well, the good-looking ones always get claimed first." Brother had an excuse for everything. Asshole.

"Since when has that ever bothered you? How many times have you simply crooked your finger and they have left whoever they were standing beside to get a ride on the Gage train?"

Rolling his eyes he said, "Just come the fuck on."

"Jesus he sounds pussy fucking whipped already." Savage chuckled as he stood beside Zeke and Lincoln.

"Thinking there's a certain woman he wants to see." Zeke chimed in.

"Fuck off. Let's fucking go." All the while Gage was grumbling out to the bikes I couldn't help but chuckle.

The moment we walked into the club I saw Gage scanning the club with a keen eye. And when I saw the man's face freeze, I looked to where his eyes were now narrowed. Damn.

I'd hightail my ass over here to see that too.

"Who is she? Think she wants a wild night with a real man." Savage quipped.

But the normal laid-back man that we all knew Gage to be turned his stare to Savage and gave him a glare that I knew, withered his balls.

"Leave. Her. The. Fuck. Alone." Gage bit out.

"Let's go sit." Lincoln said as we made our way while the crowd parted to let us by over to one of the two reserved booths.

The moment we had sat down the woman in question walked up to our table with a pad in her hand as she pulled a pencil out from behind her ear.

"Conleigh, how you doin' darlin'?" Gage asked her softly.

"Gage. Fine." The beauty replied.

"Told you I'd help. Don't want you working at a place like this." The moment he said that all of our attention moved from the woman to Gage.

"I know and I really do appreciate it, Gage, but Collins needs more treatments. What I make just isn't enough." The woman sounded tired.

Gage started to say, "Done told…."

"Gage, please. I'm hanging on by a thread here. Don't start." She took a breath and then she smiled at all of us, "What can I get y'all to drink?"

Around the table, we gave her our orders.

The moment she walked off I asked, "The fuck is up with that?"

"When she was seventeen she created a software program that she sold and made millions. Then at eighteen, she created another program and the same thing happened. Her sister, the fucking bitch, got pregnant and didn't want to keep the baby. Conleigh went to bat for that baby. Not exactly sure how she managed it all, but she was granted guardianship over Collins. Then at twenty-one, she was able to adopt her niece. When her sister, Hazel had the baby, as soon as she had her, I'm talking like within six hours, she left the hospital against medical advice, they haven't seen nor heard from her since. What is pretty cool is that if you put a picture of Hazel and Conleigh side by side with Collins, she looks more like Conleigh."

He stopped talking when the woman, Conleigh, brought our drinks over.

The moment she walked away he continued. "Seven months ago Collins was diagnosed with leukemia. During the day, Conleigh works on programs and at night she works here then after her shift she sleeps at the hospital with Collins. Collins is at the hospital in the children's ward right now fighting. I go up there twice a week and read to her. And before you ask, how do I know all of this, they're my neighbors."

When Powers had told us one morning that Gage was excused from Church two days a week, we had all wanted to know. But now that I understood, I made a mental note to let Powers know that I would be on the rotation.

I had just taken a sip of my whiskey when I looked up and froze.

Sitting on one of the barstools was that all too familiar long blonde hair. It's been seven years and I can only imagine that she has gotten even prettier with age. That was just her. Michelle.

Placing my glass back on the table, I stood, straightened my kutte then I waded through the patrons until I was ten feet behind her.

Walking up behind her I ran everything over in my mind on what I was going to say. I knew the first words to come out of my mouth were going to be, I'm sorry.

I had just stepped up behind her when she turned her head and I felt the excitement that I had been feeling wash away.

"Well hello there handsome." The woman that was most assuredly not Michelle said saucily.

Shaking my head I said, "Sorry, thought you were someone else."

"Well, I can be whoever you want me to be." She purred as she brought her hand up to place it on my chest.

Stepping back reflexively I offered her a small grin, "Appreciate it honey, but even though you're a mighty fine woman, you're not the woman I'm looking for."

I ignored her huff of outrage as I walked back to our booth. I didn't give a fuck.

As soon as my ass hit the booth, I knew that they weren't going to say a goddamn thing to me. They all knew about the woman that I would give every breath in my body to see again.

So with Powers' blessing, two weeks later I sat there beside Collin's hospital bed as I read one of my favorite books to her, *Percy Jackson and the Last Olympians.*

After I finished reading the second chapter to her I saw her eyelids drooping, I leaned down and placed a kiss on her temple.

Her next words stopped me in my tracks, I didn't even bother to correct her.

"Thanks, Uncle Cam."

"Welcome sweet pea. I'll see you Thursday." I told her softly as I placed the book on her little nightstand and then left the room.

Furious at all the assholes that had kids when they had no intention of being there for them when they needed them. Besides Gage, Collins and Conleigh had just found another person at their backs.

You never know how dirty a song's lyrics are… until you hear a child sing them.

-Laci singing Garth Brook's song *That Summer*

Chapter 2

Michelle

As soon as that second hand hit the twelve on the clock above the nurse's station I all but hauled ass to the monitor to clock out. This day had been one for the books. Thank God it was over and I didn't have to come back for two whole days.

I hadn't told Laci that yet, but I knew she was going to be ecstatic.

I had covered for a fellow PA four days ago and he had switched days with me. I didn't know how to feel about having a Saturday and a Sunday off. Working twelve-hour shifts was hectic but I loved it.

Ever since we had moved back to Dogwood from Cincinnati six months ago; I had my mom drop Laci off at school and pick her up when I couldn't get her.

We had repaired the rift between us the same week I had left and moved in with my Aunt Mae. My mother wasn't happy about it, but she understood, and I was forever grateful for that fact.

Therefore, the moment Laci saw my truck pulling into the parking lot at her school, she jumped up from where she was sitting on a bench and all but ran to me.

Laughing as one of the teachers ran after her to open the right-side passenger truck door.

"Laci, girl. What are we to do with you." Ms. Abrams the guidance counselor chided.

"When it comes to my momma, nothing." Ms. Abrams offered me a kind smile as she waved then closed the back door.

"Have a good day sweet pea?"

"Yep. You'll never guess what happened. So, Cindy was on the monkey bars and guess who was below her so he could catch her in case she fell?"

"I don't know. Who?"

"Cort." I smiled as I remembered the little dreamy look in her eyes as she always talked about Cort.

"Yeah?"

"It was so cute and sweet. Mommy, do I go after him now, or let him be?"

"Honey, you're six years old. Why are you talking about going after boys?"

"You taught me that we only live once. We have to make the best of the life we are given."

Damn. Who knew a six-year-old could outsmart someone. "I think you need to wait for when that person walks in your life and you get butterflies in your tummy and your heartbeat picks up to match the rhythm of theirs."

Nothing more was said as I pulled away from the curb.

As soon as I pulled out of the primary school where Laci had enrolled in six months ago one of my favorite songs came on. We had the windows rolled down and together my daughter and I had joined in with the song.

Just as we both sang the lyrics, *To watch a storm with all its wonder raging in her lover's eye. She had to ride the heat of passion like a comet burning bright.* My face flushed.

It took everything in me to not change the song, I made a mental note to never play this song again while my daughter was in hearing distance.

As soon as Laci and I got home, she ran for something while I changed. The moment I walked back into the living room in some comfortable sweats it was to see that Laci had grabbed our manicure bag.

We painted our fingernails and toenails. I was now sporting rainbow nail polish. I would have to take the polish off come Monday morning but for the weekend I was repping the polish.

We had just sat down in front of our tv to have pizza and a movie night when Laci asked, "Mommy, have you ever gotten butterflies in your tummy and your heartbeat matched another's?"

I made a vow the day I had Laci that I would never lie to her. Not ever.

So pulling my big girl panties up so to speak, I answered her, "Yes. Once."

"And what happened?"

"Don't talk with your mouth full young lady." I teased her as I did the same thing.

Laughing, I sobered. "You know about that night baby." She had asked me when she was five where her daddy was. That day at school, they had been making father's day presents. So because of that vow, I told her the truth.

I knew I should shield her from things like that, but I never wanted to lie to my daughter. Lies hurt.

"Yes, mommy. And I know you hate the man that did that to you but you are thankful that you have me."

"That's right baby, always will be." Sitting my slice down on my plate I turned to face her. "I met the man that gave me butterflies and that caused my heart to beat, not for me, but for him. I laid eyes on him when I was fourteen years old and I just knew. I knew he was the man that I was meant to be with. That night had happened because a lie was told to him, and he believed the other woman over me. I had run out of the clubhouse, crushed, and I didn't pay attention to my surroundings."

"So, you really should be telling that guy thank you because had that not happened you wouldn't have me." Six-year-olds and their logic.

"When did you get so smart?"

"Mommy, that's because I have you flowing through my veins."

"Love you sweet pea."

"Love you too mommy. Have you ever seen him again after that night?"

"No, to be honest, I hadn't wanted to take the position at the hospital because his clubhouse is here.

"Clubhouse? What is that?"

"He is or was in a motorcycle club." The moment those words came out of my mouth Laci looked up at me wide-eyed.

Shrieking, she asked, "He was in a motorcycle club?"

"Yes, baby. He was. Just like your grandpa, same club."

"Then before that night, he was a good man. I'll kick him in the shin for you if I ever see him."

Laughing softly, I placed a kiss atop her raven black hair and then turned my attention back to the movie that we watched a thousand times, *How To Train Your Dragon*. My daughter didn't like Hiccup. No, she liked Astrid.

The next morning the moment we woke up I drove her two towns over to a huge flea market that I hadn't been to in years. Not since Cameron, had taken me.

We walked up and down the aisles taking everything in. The moment we passed by a certain booth, Laci pulled my hand over to one of them, "Mommy, look at it."

I smiled at the woman that had a stand set up with bracelets. "These are beautiful."

"These are so cool. Do you have a kit or something?" Laci asked excitedly.

"Sure do." The woman smiled down at my daughter as she bent to grab a kit underneath her table.

"Wow. This is cool." The moment Laci grabbed the kit she had a gigantic smile on her face.

"How much?"

She winked then said, "Ten."

Grinning, I pulled a ten from my back pocket and handed it over to the lady.

Then my eyes landed on a pair of blue friendship bracelets. Buying those, I knelt down in front of Laci.

"Be my best friend forever." Her cute little giggle was what I lived for.

"Yes!" Smiling, I put the bracelet on her wrist while she did the same for me.

"Cute little girl." A man said as we stood up.

My back straightened as I pulled Laci into my embrace before I looked over at the man.

He was like a glass of water in the Mojave desert. Geez, he was beautiful. His hair was cut close to his scalp and he had a beard that was awesome. Ink ran up and down his arms. He wasn't built per se but he had a swimmer's body all lean with muscle.

Even though he was beautiful, sadly he did nothing for me. No one had since Cameron. Shaking my head out of that train wreck of a thought I took in his kutte.

"Can I see the back of your kutte?" The man's brows crinkled as he shrugged then offered me his back. Letting out a slow breath I loosened my hold on Laci.

The man turned back around as he asked, "Okay?"

"Yeah. Sorry. I'm a bit overprotective." I offered him unapologetically.

"No better way to be. I'm Lincoln."

"Michelle. This is Laci with an I." I always had to say that. To more people than I can count.

"Nice to meet you both." He grinned then looked down at Laci nodding at the kit in her hands, "You going to make some of those?"

"Yep. I think they are cool." She smiled up at him.

He nodded then turned his head to look at something, then said, "Alright. Y'all have a good day."

Nodding, we turned and continued down the aisle of vendors. The moment we walked away from the man Laci asked in a whisper, "Was that him?"

"No baby. That wasn't him. But he's in the same motorcycle club."

"Good. I didn't want to mess up my shoes." Tossing my head back I laughed full out. She was wearing little pink ballet flats with sparkles on them.

Sunday night after dinner with my mother I read Laci a bedtime story then crawled into bed and like a light, I was out.

Dreams of how things used to be with Cameron filled my sleep.

What's long, hard, and has cum in it?

Cucumber. But I like the way you think.

Chapter 3

Cam

"What's up brother, you alright?" I asked Lincoln as he walked over to where I stood with Savage. He had a weird look on his face that I have never seen before.

"Yeah, just think I found Mrs. Right." Lincoln stood there looking off in the distance.

"Oh shit. Another one bites the dust." Savage started to sing.

"Shut the fuck up." I chuckled as Lincoln punched Savage in the shoulder.

"What was her name?" I asked, intrigued.

"I'm not telling. All the good ones get claimed before I get to them." Lincoln said as we all started walking to our bikes.

As soon as we walked into the clubhouse Powers called out, "Church."

One by one we dropped our phones into the bowl outside of the double doors.

The moment we were all in our chairs with Powers at the head of the table, myself to his right across from Gage. Heathen sat to my left, while Savage sat across from him. Beside him was Lincoln, then across from him was Zeke. Greek sat across from him with Clutch on the opposite end. And at the end of the table was Skinner.

With the sound of the gavel being hit on the table, everyone quieted down.

"Where are we on builds?"

"Three weeks ahead of schedule," I told him. Smirking. We had all been busting our asses.

Powers looked relieved when he said, "Thank fuck. Let's get a month ahead then we are all going on fucking vacation." Knocks from fists sounded on the table.

"How are the books?" Powers took a puff off of his cigarette. He had been cutting back, only smoking one in church. He never smoked in front of or near his kids.

Lincoln rolled in his chair to the safe and pulled out the books. For the next twenty minutes, we went over all of the income that we have coming in from our businesses and the expenses that we have.

"Security?" Powers looked at Greek.

Greek said, "Nothing's hitting my end. All of our Doves have reported to their handlers for their check-ins."

"Fucking good. Does anyone need to bring anything to the table"

"Well not really, except Lincoln says that he met Mrs. Right." Rounds of chuckles came from us as Savage opened his big ass mouth.

"And I'm not sharing that shit. Soon as a good woman comes in all y'all vultures will be on her like white on rice."

"Well, you can exclude Powers, Heathen, Skinner, and Cam. See the odds are better in your favor." Savage quipped.

Skinner wouldn't make a move on anyone. No, he had been changed irrevocably. As for why I wouldn't make a move, none of them was the woman that I wanted.

Just as Powers' opened his mouth to say something, the church doors were opened as Lil stormed in. We all watched with bated breath wondering what he had done this time.

With angry stomps, she walked to Powers, leaned in, and placed her finger in his face, "You are the biggest shit head known to man. How could you tell Rosa that it was okay to eat all the cake she wanted?"

"Darlin' it's her birthday tomorrow…"

"That's not my point you shit head. You told her and I quote, what does it matter if your butt gets big like your momma? She's freaking beautiful."

Around the room, everyone sat frozen until none of us could hold the laughter back anymore. I heard one of my brothers murmur, "We need to bring fucking popcorn in here."

"Baby…" He tried.

"Don't you baby me. Your ass just lost my mouth in the mornings." With that, she turned and stormed out.

Without banging the gavel, Powers stood and stormed after her. Lil was the one thing in this world that could bring our president to his knees. Which she did without even batting an eyelash.

I was holding my stomach because I was laughing so hard. Hell even Skinner sat at the end of the room shaking his head.

"Well, I'm guessing church is dismissed." I was still laughing as I banged the gavel on the oak table.

Just as I was walking out of church and heading to the front double doors of the clubhouse Lincoln came up to my side.

"You wanna know what's odd?" With that comment, I stopped and looked at him.

"What's that?"

"Said her name was Michelle and had a daughter." With that, he walked off.

Standing there in the open doorway I let my jaw work, I wasn't going to get my hopes up. Every single curly-haired blonde beauty that was the right height I had approached over the past six years, hoping beyond hope that it was her, that she had finally come back where she belonged.

Shaking my head I walked to the garage to get started on a few builds that we had due in about three weeks, thank fuck we were that far ahead.

We had to turn down builds two years ago and we were finally catching up.

Two hours later just as I tightened a bolt down, I saw Heathen storm to his bike as he roared out of the compound.

It was then that Powers walked into the garage shaking his head. "What's up?"

"Heathen's boys were playing in the backyard, fucking hellions. They fell out of the tree. Taking them to the hospital now."

Without another word we all got on our bikes and headed to the hospital. Ignoring the fact that we had grease all over us.

The moment we made it to their room it was to hear June laying into her boys. Momma didn't hold punches with her boys.

"Momma told you not to be climbing shit," Heathen told his boys.

"Boys," Skinner said as he looked down at both of the boys. Only then did they look down.

"Darlin'. You okay?" It was something else to see Skinner show any affection to anyone, but he showed that side of him to June as he wrapped an arm around her shoulders.

"Yeah Skinner. Just scared me to death when I heard their screams. Something I never want to hear again."

Releasing her, she went to Heathen as he wrapped his arms around her. "We are just waiting on the results from the doctor. We know they each broke an arm."

"What's the verdict?" June asked as the doctor stepped inside, then froze at seeing all of us in their hospital room.

"Umm… well…" The damn doctor was sweating.

"Doc ain't no one here going to hurt you." Powers sighed. Lil turned her face into Powers' chest as her body shook with silent laughter.

As if he was in a speech contest he said as fast as he could, "Nathan broke the ulna in his right arm. And Lucas broke the radius in his left arm. They will both be getting casts today and in about four to six weeks if the bones have healed properly we can take the casts off."

After about thirty minutes the Doc returned with what he needed to cast both of their arms.

They had wrapped Nathan's arm in a red cast and Lucas's arm in a blue cast. What had me laughing my ass off were the glares that the boys sent to the doc. "Can't you make them multi-colored? You know, like the American flag or something?" Nathan asked.

"I'm sorry but we can't do that." Heathen stood there with a proud smile on his face.

"Alright brother, y'all need me, let me know," I told them as I turned to walk out of the hospital room.

"Go chop that fucking tree down," Heathen growled out.

"Don't you dare. They are your kids, what did you expect?" June chided him.

Shaking my head in laughter I headed down the hall and the elevator that would take me to the main entrance.

Just as I stepped off the elevator from visiting Nathan and Lucas my breath stalled in my lungs. No way. No fucking way.

I don't have an attitude problem!

You just get on my damn nerves!!

Chapter 4

Michelle

Today has been a shitty day. The first thing to make this day so horrible was that I had forgotten to set my alarm clock, but thankfully Laci was an early riser.

So I hadn't been able to straighten nor tame my unruly curly hair. Today I just threw a clip in it and allowed all my curls to bounce free.

The second thing to happen after I dropped Laci off at school was that the moment I pulled up at the hospital there had been a bad accident this morning on the highway. They really needed to add more lights and people needed to obey them also when a light changes to yellow, you slow the fuck down not speed up. Do they know that red means to stop? Apparently not.

So many lives' have been lost because of stupid bastards like that. Take their license away and be done with it.

I was in my own head trying to calm my breaths when I had to call time of death on a five-year-old little boy who had been in the back seat when an angry driver didn't like that the mother of said little boy was obeying the law.

It wasn't her fault that the driver had been in a rush. Would I be imprisoned if I put something into his IV that made his heart stop as retribution? Probably, would it be worth it? Most definitely.

If I didn't have Laci, I would have done it.

"Michelle? Is that really you?" Everything in my mind froze as a voice I haven't heard in years but only in my dreams spoke from behind me.

Don't you do it, Michelle, you keep on walking. Don't you dare look back at him. Had another position opened up anywhere else in the continental U.S. I would have jumped on it.

"Michelle," he whispered.

Sighing, I turned around to look up at the man that broke my heart all those years ago. The man that left me when I needed him the most. The one and only time when I was scared out of my mind. Literally.

Damn did he age good. My God, he was breathtaking. His hair was the same, his eyes were the same. He now sported a beard that would feel great as he moved his mouth all over my skin, get a grip girl. All of his looks did nothing to hide the fact that his heart was black.

"Cameron," I nodded. There was something in his eyes when I called him Cameron, but just like that, he wiped it away. I wasn't the one to make that choice, he was.

"You work here now?" He asked as he took in my white lab coat.

"Yes, as of about six months ago." Placing my hands in my coat so he wouldn't see that they were trembling.

"What do you do?" His hands were in his pockets and I noticed that he had hunched his shoulders in on himself, so as to not scare me with how much bigger he had gotten.

Two of my thighs resembled one of his, and let's face it, I was no longer a size four, no my ass only fit in a size ten now.

I had been determined to lose my baby weight after I had Laci but then I had said screw it and I embraced my new curves.

Sure, I got looks everywhere I went and I was flattered, but I've never allowed anyone past first base. If I was being honest, I didn't even allow them to be on the roster.

"I work in the emergency room for now. One day I plan on getting my doctorate and working in general pediatrics medicine."

"Wow. You always talked about it, glad to see you've made it. How come you didn't go all the way."

Before I could reply to him, Mackenzie walked up, "Ms. O'Connell here are the files from the other hospital."

"Thank you, Mackenzie." After she walked away I looked up at Cameron and said, "Good to see you." See, I could use the manners that my mom and my aunt taught me.

Turning from him I started to walk away then heard, "Have coffee with me after your shift."

"Can't I have plans." Turning back around I walked to the nurse's station.

The rest of the day was filled with Cameron Titus Bryant. The bastard. Just like that six years later, and he was still all I could think about.

Thankfully, the moment I picked Laci up from after-school care, my mind was filled with her and her only.

What would I do without her? Where would I be? I didn't even want to think about it.

We had just gotten our order of food at Calhoun's when I noticed a shadow fall over our table. Looking up it was to see Cameron standing there. He was staring at Laci.

I could tell that he saw the resemblance between the two of them, it was something that had floored me when I first laid eyes on Laci when they had placed her on my chest. Shaking his head he turned his attention back to me, "Michelle."

Nodding, "Cameron."

"Who is this?" He asked me as he looked back over at Laci.

"This is my daughter Laci." I bit my lip when I saw fury flare in his eyes. We had talked about children too. He knew that I had wanted to have two kids. And all of them too have him as their father. He also knew what names I wanted them to have too.

Strange how what we want to work out never really does. And sometimes, like with my daughter, things worked out even better.

"Let me guess, Laci with an I right?" He remembered that?

"Good guess. How did you know?" Laci chimed in.

"Your momma told me if she ever had a girl, that was what she would name her."

"That's so cool," Laci said as she dipped her fry in a mixture of ketchup and mayo.

Cameron smirked when she did that, "Damn just like her momma."

I held in the grin that wanted to come forth as I did the same thing.

"Y'all having a mommy-daughter date?"

"Yes. About three times a week if I'm not on shift." I answered him.

Laci decided then that she was going to get to know this man that was a stranger to her but that had never been a stranger to me, well until that night, "Do you ride a motorcycle?"

"I do." His attention was solely on her and my insides quivered.

"How fast does it go?"

"Depends on the road."

"Really?"

"Yeah. Dirt road, about thirty miles an hour, flat top with no cracks, about one fifteen, one twenty."

Her eyes were wide when she asked, "Can I go for a ride?"

"Long as your momma okays it and you get a little bigger."

"Cool. I'll work on her. Do you have any brothers?" Shaking my head I took a bite of my burger.

"I do." It was then that he turned and pointed to some other men in the far corner of the restaurant. "They aren't my brothers by blood but they are my brothers."

"I gotcha. Kind of like Callie and her mommy."

His brows furrowed as he asked, "What do you mean?"

"Callie's mommy isn't her real mommy, she's her step mommy but Callie won't call the woman that gave birth to her mom."

He nodded in understanding, "Yeah just like that."

What shocked me was not once did Cameron get irritated with her questions. Normally when a six-year-old starts asking questions people get annoyed, but not Cameron.

It was then that he pulled his phone out of his back pocket and checked the display. I saw his jaw tighten as he looked at me, "Gotta run. It was good to see you." He said to me then turned his gaze to Laci, "Nice to meet you peanut."

With that, he walked away. And damn if I didn't watch his behind the entire way.

"Mommy, that was him, wasn't it?" Her head was turned as she watched Cameron walk to the hostess station and then left.

"Yes sweet pea, that was him."

"I look like him. Don't I?" She wasn't the only one that saw that. She should have been his.

If only he would have listened to me, "Yes baby, you do."

When the waitress brought us to-go cups, I asked for the check.

"No need. Y'alls meal has already been covered." I wasn't going to get mad at the waitress; she was only doing her job. But I was going to get mad at Cameron.

However that night after Laci went to bed, I didn't even try to keep the tears at bay.

I had thought that Laci had gone to sleep. Though that wasn't the case.

I felt her climb on my bed as she wrapped her little arms around my neck and held me while I cried.

"I got you, mommy. I love you."

"I love you too, sweet pea so very much."

"Do you want to give him another chance?"

"I don't know, baby."

"Well, you always tell me to look for the good in people and not the bad." My six-year-old is turning things around on me.

Chuckling, I unwrapped from her and pulled her in my arms as I grabbed the remote and started Frozen for her.

Within minutes she was sound asleep, I was the only one that was still wide awake as the credits rolled on the screen.

What was I going to do?

Don't be so hard on yourself.

The mom in E.T. had an alien living in her house for days,

and she never even noticed.

Chapter 5

Cam

Seeing that little girl ate me up inside, knowing that had I not made Michelle leave, then she would have paid more attention to her surroundings and she wouldn't have been raped by that mother fucker. Hell, she wouldn't have walked to her fucking car alone.

Michelle had been raised in a home that babies were miracles, no matter how they were conceived, so I knew she wouldn't have an abortion.

What struck me was how much the little girl looked like my mother. That was insane.

Not only that but I didn't miss the resemblance to the face that I stared at every morning in the mirror. If that wasn't a kick in the balls I didn't know what was.

I sighed when I looked up and saw one of the club whores making her way over to me, why did Flo feel the need to talk to me. How many times had I already shot her down?

"Hey, Cam.."

"Done told you, you don't have the right to call me that. It's Cameron."

"But I don't understand, everyone calls you Cam."

"Then you haven't been paying attention. My brothers, their ole' ladies, and their kids have that right. No one else."

"Ugh... fine, then what is it gonna take to get you to allow me to call you Cam?"

"Flattered honey but I'm not interested." She should be used to this by now. It was always the same answer I had given her time and time again.

"You never are. What is it going to take?"

"For you to be someone else," I told her honestly.

"Well, what do I need to look like?" Was she serious?

Laughing darkly, I said, "It's not just that Flo. Yes, you're very pretty, but you're not her. You could put on twenty pounds, change your hair type and color, hell even wear a different perfume, but you wouldn't be her."

"Sometimes you have to let go of something to receive something even more beautiful."

"In a way, you're right Flo. But when you find your soulmate, there is no letting go of that. There's nothing beyond that."

Either she sensed that this conversation wasn't going the way she wanted or she just finally understood where my head and my heart was at. I sighed, thankfully, that she turned on her spiked heels and walked away.

"What's on your mind?" I looked over to see that Lil had sat down beside me in one of the loungers that we had around the fire pit.

Sighing, I asked, "You hear about the girl I broke up with then the moment she left here was raped?"

"Yes. Everyone knows about that." Sadness was written all over her features.

"The girl is back," I told her with my head hung low.

Her breath hitched in her throat as she asked, "She came back?"

"Yep. Now she wants nothing to do with me." And truth be told I couldn't say that I blamed her.

"You haven't seen her since that night right? She probably just needs time. Thank God I've never had to deal with something like that and I hope and pray that I never have to. But those memories are probably playing havoc with her emotions."

"I've only seen her twice but still, before she left town, she would have talked to me until my ears bled."

"Cam, I know you. I also know that you haven't even been with another woman. Tell her that. Make her see

50

you. Wear her down." I kept replaying Lil's words over and over in my head for the next two days.

I called the hospital to see when she was going to be on shift next. I was fucking lucky when they told me that she was scheduled for lunch in an hour.

Thankfully, I had time to grab us some lunch as I headed to the hospital.

The moment I parked my bike and grabbed the bag out of my saddlebags I started for the emergency room department.

Having a lot of nurses' eyes on me didn't faze me in the slightest. They weren't the eyes that I wanted on me.

However the moment I walked up to the nurse's station I saw that wealth of familiar blonde hair.

Grinning, I walked over to her and muttered, "Beautiful."

I smiled when I saw her back straighten then when she slowly turned around her eyes had narrowed. "Cameron."

"Michelle. Lunch?" Smiling, I held up the bag.

"I'm not hungry." However, her stomach had betrayed that lie when it grumbled.

Smirking, I asked, "You sure about that?"

I saw her head lower as she shook it. "Let's go."

Hiding the smile that wanted so badly to burst forth I followed her through the emergency room while I heard whispers at my back. It didn't deter me though; no way was I letting this opportunity pass me by.

The moment we made it to the cafeteria, I followed her to a corner table.

She took the chair that was open to the room, leaving the one that was against the wall for me, "You remembered." I muttered.

"Just like you remembered what I love from that place." Thankfully they had paper towel dispensers on every table.

"Busted." I knew she knew what I got her; it was hard to miss that smell of the barbeque.

Sitting the plates down on the table. I handed her the fork and grabbed my own. "So how come you're only a PA and not a doctor?"

She sighed, "Laci. I wanted to give her everything I could without taking time away from her."

"I get that. Do you plan to go after your doctorate?"

"Yes, when she gets a little older." She said as she took another bite of her barbeque.

She had just grabbed a napkin to wipe her mouth as she looked down at the table and whispered, "That man. That attacked me. Any clue where he is? I filed the police report but his DNA wasn't in the system."

"You don't need to worry about him."

As soon as those words left my mouth she looked up at me with shock written all over her face, "You mean…"

"Mean, he's enjoying his long-extended life in hell."

Her shoulders relaxed as she whispered, "Thanks, Cameron."

"Think you can call me Cam?"

"No. I wasn't the one to draw that line, Cameron, you were." With that said she grabbed the trash and stood. "Thanks for lunch Cameron. I needed that."

And with that, I watched her ass in those scrubs as she walked away.

I've seen women in barely there clothing, leaving nothing to the imagination, but seeing Michelle in a pair of scrubs, my dick was hard within seconds.

Two weeks later after driving to the hospital every day she had lunch and spending an hour with her at a time, I had a plan in place and this time I was getting some fucking answers.

***

Michelle

As soon as I stepped outside of the hospital, inhaled the fresh air, this was by far my favorite time of the day.

Breathing in the smell that was in a hospital wasn't in my top ten.

The moment I made it to my truck I halted in my tracks. There sitting on his bike beside my truck was Cameron. "Go for a ride with me?"

"I gotta get Laci from her after-school program."

"Couple of the brothers and their ladies are going for a ride, one of them is pregnant so she is staying at the clubhouse, she's watching the kids. I know the other kids would like to play with Laci."

Swallowing I said, "Not sure I can go back to that clubhouse Cameron."

I stood there for a few moments as he thought about it, then I watched as he grabbed his phone and placed a call "Yeah, y'all at home?"

"Yeah, y'all mind watching Michelle's daughter for a few hours?"

Nodding he said, "Cool see you in a few."

After he hung up he said, "Heathen and June can watch her. Is she okay with dogs?"

"Umm yea she is." What was I doing?

"Let's go get her, then y'all can follow me to their place and you can leave your car there."

"Cameron. I just don't know."

"I know you're scared Michelle, but please just give me this if nothing else. Come for a ride with me, Michelle. No one has ever been on the back of my bike before. Help me break that cherry."

Normally that statement about the cherry would have caused me to go into a panic attack but coming from him, it didn't.

Knowing he would just keep pushing until I caved, nodding. "Okay."

"Just text me their address and I'll meet you there. I gotta run home and change."

"Okay."

Twenty minutes later I was turning off the main road and onto a paved driveway. Laci had asked for my phone so she could take pictures.

"Oh my God. Mommy look at all the dogs." Grinning at her excitement I took the dogs in and was amazed that none of them tried to get close to the truck but a few of them were barking. There were only three of them but to Laci's little body, that was a lot.

When we made it to a house upon a little incline, I saw Cameron standing there on the porch with a man and a woman along with two kids.

Those two kids each had a cast on an arm. "Remember your manners okay?"

"Yes, mommy." Getting out of the truck and rounding the hood, I helped her down out of the truck.

Holding her hand as we made it up the front walk, "Cameron!" She squealed. "Mommy told me you were going to take her for a ride."

"That's right, peanut. Did you help her dress?" He asked as he eyed my boots, jeans, and my thick sweater.

"Nope. But I did tell her that she looked pretty." Which she had done the moment I stepped from my bedroom.

"Good job peanut." He smiled down at her then looked at me, "This is June and Heathen and their sons Nathan and Lucas."

I held my hand out for June and nodded at Heathen, the man was intense, so intense that I could feel a protective barrier coming from him. That I would respect.

"It's nice to meet you too."

With the introductions done, the little boy that I had been introduced as Nathan asked Laci, "Do you like dogs?"

"Yes. We can't have one because mommy works a lot but I love them."

"Come on, we can introduce you to them." They both looked so much like their dad that it was uncanny. Seeing June's smaller stature standing beside Heathen, I wondered how she managed to carry both of the boys.

I called to Laci's back as she followed the two boys, "Have fun baby. I love you."

Running after the boys she turned her head as she yelled, "Love you too mommy."

***

Cameron

Grabbing the helmet I had bought for her in town I handed it to her. She stilled; I knew that she saw the design. It was a flower design in her favorite color, blue.

"You bought this for me?" I saw the hesitation in her eyes.

"Yeah. Not going to have you on the back of my bike without a helmet baby." Her eyes flared when I called her baby, she just needed to get over that fact.

The moment she climbed on behind me, wrapped her arms around my waist, I inhaled a breath. She was a wet dream.

"Hold on tight," I told her, and she squeezed her arms around my waist.

We made it down the driveway and out of town, but instead of meeting with the club, I drove around on the backroads. The moment we had turned down one backroad that would take us by a lake, I felt her body shaking, laughter bubbled up out of her which caused me to smile.

We had just pulled into the driveway of Heathen's place to see Laci playing with a couple of the dogs. "Did you like the ride?"

"Yes, loved it. Now I get why people ride motorcycles." Her cheeks were flushed. She was fucking breathtaking.

She took her helmet off and handed it to me, shaking my head at her, I said, "Keep it. It's yours."

I saw a range of emotions assault her features, but everything was let go when Laci came running over to us.

"Thank you so much for watching her. I had a blast." The soft smile on Michelle's face had me clenching my fists to stop me from pulling her into my embrace and slamming my mouth down on hers.

"Of course! Any time." June smiled back at her.

"Mommy those dogs are so pretty."

"That they are." She said as she rubbed one of them behind its ears.

I smiled down at one who had followed Laci to where we stood. "You have a good time, peanut?"

"Yes. They are two grades ahead of me, but they told me during recess that we could all play together."

"Good I won't have to worry about anyone being mean to you." I tapped her nose with my index finger. Her giggle was music to my ears.

After she got Laci loaded up in her truck I said, "Come on I'll follow y'all home."

This feeling in the pit of my stomach that shit needed to be ironed out, couldn't be overlooked anymore.

All my life I thought air was free.

Until I bought a bag of chips.

Chapter 6

Michelle

Laci had fallen asleep and before I could get her out of the truck, there was Cameron. I felt his hands on my waist as he moved me to the side, unbuckled her seatbelt, then ever so carefully, he gathered her in his arms.

Shutting the door, we walked up the front walk. Unlocking the front door, I led him to Laci's bedroom.

Before I could help, he used one hand as he turned her covers back and laid her down on her bed.

The moment he placed a kiss on her temple, I felt parts of my heart that have long since been dead, start to waken. Nope. No way.

"Thank you," I whispered as I walked to my fridge and grabbed a beer, holding it out to him, he nodded as he tagged it from me. Grabbing my own we walked to the front porch.

Sitting down in the porch swing, it didn't even groan, but the moment Cameron followed suit, it did.

As the crickets sang in the night air I took a swig of my beer.

I could feel emotions that I couldn't decipher coming from Cameron. Breaking the silence he asked, "What is it going to take Michelle? I've done everything I can think of to get you to see the man that I am today?"

I had been weighing the options on what I should and shouldn't do. However, everything came back to one thing. I was going to hell. Straight there.

Then when I opened my mouth and told him what I wanted, to say that I was shocked at the statement that followed was an understatement.

"I want you to fuck me. I want you to fuck me so hard that I can't breathe. Slam me against the wall and make me forget that night all those years ago. I want it to happen in my house after Laci goes to sleep. I don't want any emotional attachments because that time is long gone."

"I'll take you anyway I can get you, and if this is how you want it, then fine. But be warned, beautiful, I'm playing for keeps. For the both of you."

And with that, he pulled out his phone and handed it to me, "Put your number in it. I'll call when I'm on my way over tomorrow night. What time does Laci go to bed at night?"

I did as he asked, then my mouth worked before my mind could tell it not to. "Nine."

"Gotcha Beautiful. Text you when I'm on my way." Grinning, he handed me his empty beer bottle and with that, he walked to his bike then pulled out of the driveway leaving me sitting there replaying our conversation on my front porch.

I needed to be put in a mental institution. Was I really considering this?

I haven't been with anyone of my choosing ever. The one and only time I had experienced sex was a horrible, nightmare of a reality.

The next day I had just read Laci a bedtime story, when I read the next sentence I noticed that she was dead to the world.

Carefully I stood from her bed, placed the book on her bedside table, then turned the tank light off to Sparks, her crested gecko, walked out of her bedroom, closing the door softly behind me.

Ten minutes later while I sat on my front porch in my swing with a beer in my hand my phone pinged with a text.

Unknown – *Be there in five.*

Michelle – *Ok...*

Exactly five minutes later Cameron pulled up to my house on his bike, the moment he turned onto my driveway he turned the bike off and then walked it up the drive. "She's loud, didn't want to wake Laci."

And with those words, the guarded wall I had around my heart fucking cracked. Did I try to stop it? That would be a no? Why? Because I was still that naïve little

62

girl that read fairy tales to my daughter and believed that true love did exist.

He was slowly working his way back under my skin and I didn't know what I was going to do when he got there fully again.

What I did know was that my guard was going to be up, but I didn't know for how long.

Taking his helmet off, he walked up the porch steps, getting off the swing I walked into the house, as he followed me.

Reaching my bedroom I turned and stood as I watched him saunter into my room.

Entering the bedroom he turned and locked the door.

Then without a moment of hesitation, he stalked over to me, wrapped me in his arms, and slammed his mouth down on mine.

I moaned in his mouth when our tongues finally danced together. I wasn't going to let anything that happens tonight go to my head. That would completely undo me and it would shatter the world that I had built for myself and Laci from nothing but tattered ashes.

When he pulled away I almost whimpered, that was until he removed his kutte, hung it on the doorknob then locked eyes with me as he hunched his shoulders, gripped the collar of this t-shirt, and ripped it from his body.

My eyes roamed his chest, lingering on the tattoo that rested over his heart, then my eyes moved lower until my brain caught up with what it had seen.

Like a rocket, my eyes shot back up to the tattoo.

Stepping closer to him with his arms now at his side, I looked at the tattoo, my breath catching in my lungs. Lifting one finger to trail it over the design I held my breath.

"Does that say what I think it says?" I asked him in a whisper.

His hands came to rest on my hips as he buried his nose in my hair, "What do you think it says?"

The tattoo was black and grey. It was a biomechanical heart, where the aorta was supposed to be, there, inked on his skin was one simple word, Michelle.

I didn't notice the tears in my eyes until I felt his thumb brush them away ever so carefully.

Burying my face in his chest I broke. Crying big fat tears into his skin.

He just stood there and held me while I cried.

"Why? Why did you do it, Cameron? Why did you trust her and not me?"

"I was young and dumb baby. I'll tell you why, but not tonight. I know what I did doesn't excuse that fact but there is something I've never told you."

Lifting my tear-stained face from his chest, he brought his hand to cup the side of my face as he brought his mouth down on mine and I completely shut my brain off and just felt.

This. This is what I have been needing, craving. Just his touch.

With deft fingers he grabbed the hem of my t-shirt and pulled it over my head. We broke apart when it came off, but then our mouths collided once again.

He walked me backward to the bed and without our mouths separating we laid down on the bed.

Our hands explored each other, and then with a push from my foot, I flipped us over.

Seeing him naked in the flesh from the waist up was like looking at the cover of a fit-magazine. The man was ripped. Did he even have fat? My guess was no. His eight-pack abs. My God. I trailed my mouth down his chest and licked the lines of his abs, as goosebumps pebbled along his skin.

"Baby, take my jeans off. My dick is getting pissed, it's out of fucking room." I giggled at that and did as he asked.

Unbuttoning his pants, pulling down his zipper as my knuckles grazed along the hard length that he had, he inhaled a breath, looking up as I took his jeans off, his eyes held a fiery passion in them.

The moment his jeans were off he sprung off the bed, grabbed me around my waist, and threw me down on the bed.

With quick movements he did the same for me, leaving me in only a pink lace bra and matching panties.

"Fuck." He growled as he stood there staring at my body.

"Cameron," I whispered.

He placed his fingers in the waistband of his boxer briefs and pulled them down his legs.

My eyes traveled with the movement to see his pulsing hard cock. "Holy fuck."

He chuckled as he palmed his cock, "Is he okay for you?"

"You think?" I snapped.

Without missing a beat he let go of his cock and climbed back on the bed.

With his hands in mine, he moved them above my head as he trailed his mouth and tongue along my jaw, down my neck as he nipped and sucked.

My body was writhing beneath his. I wasn't scared. I wasn't nervous. I had time to heal. I wasn't going to punish either of us because of someone else's actions.

"Cameron, there's been no one else." I felt the need to tell him so he would know how big of a moment this was.

Lifting his eyes to mine so I could see the honesty in his blue eyes he murmured, "I haven't wanted anyone else. My dick doesn't get hard for anyone except you."

"Are you saying what I think you're saying?"

"Yeah baby, I am. You're my first and my last same with you. Some other man may have had a hand at making Laci, but baby, she's mine."

With that bomb being dropped he continued down my chest, smiling when he saw my bra had a front clasp on it.

He used one hand to unsnap my bra open as my free hand wrapped around the back of his thick corded neck.

My hips bucked up into him as his tongue circled my nipple. He nipped, licked, tugged, all the while swirling his tongue around my nipple. The sensations he was causing in my body were things that I had only ever imagined about.

Reading scenes like this in books, well that had nothing on the actual feelings that I was feeling.

After he showed the other nipple the same consideration he let his mouth wander down my body, both of my hands were free now as I grabbed the comforter in them.

"Love this." He breathed as he tongued my belly button ring. Remaining there for a few moments before his mouth moved down.

Down and down he went until I felt a gentle kiss on my pussy through my underwear.

Using his teeth, he pulled my underwear from my body, lifting my hips to help get the offending garment off my body. The moment I had one leg out, I used the other to kick them off.

His chuckle filled the room.

Snapping out of my haze I heard a phone ringing that wasn't mine, groaning. I said, "No."

"Ignore it. I am. Nothing in this world could pull me away from you." And when the phone rang again a second time he didn't stop as he trailed kisses up the insides of my thighs.

And finally, he brought his tongue to my pussy, licking up and down, he groaned. "I could live here. Fuck, your pussy tastes even better than my dreams. Like fucking honey."

He parted my lips with his tongue and then when he captured my clit in between his lips, I saw fucking stars.

"Ready?"

"Ready for what?" I asked him.

"I'm about to place my fingers in your pussy baby. Need to know if you're okay with that?" I felt tears hit my eyes yet again. My God, this man.

"Yes, Cam. I'm ready." I didn't see his face as I called him Cam, but I felt his body relax between my thighs.

And then I felt first one finger, then two enter me. He found the rhythm that my body was on and then he attacked like a starved man.

Within minutes as I felt my first ever orgasm start to hit my body his tongue was flicking my clit in time with his fingers.

And then like a shot, my back bowed off of the bed as I moaned, "Cam."

Chuckling, he helped me through my orgasm.

When my body stopped shaking he removed his mouth and his fingers.

I felt him start to crawl off the bed, but not before I watched with avid fascination as he pulled the two fingers out of my pussy and brought them to his mouth, sucking my juices from them. Was it possible to cum from that alone? Yes, it was.

He bent to his jeans and pulled something from his pocket. A condom.

"When you're ready, we won't use these fuckers anymore."

I simply nodded, not comprehending what he was saying but unable to form a response. It wouldn't be until later when I fully understood what that statement meant.

"You're already dripping for me, baby." He said as he lined his condom-covered dick with my entrance.

He brought his mouth to mine, kissing me as he started to slowly enter me. Inch by delectable inch.

My pussy stretched wide for him, filling me up so deep that I could feel it in my throat.

I felt a power pour into me like I have never felt before, "Cam."

"Yeah, baby. Yeah. Feel it too." And with that, he started to retreat, my heels dug into his back to keep him inside of me.

I shouldn't have worried though, no far from it.

He slammed back inside of me.

"Fuck you feel so fucking good. I can feel your heat through this condom."

"I feel… I feel…" I breathed out.

"I know, I won't last long. Fucckkkk." He groaned as his eyes closed for the briefest moment, and then his eyes were locked with mine.

Feeling him moving in and out of me, I lifted my head to see where our two bodies connected as one and that caused the orgasm that had been there on the verge of hitting me, to come raging out of me at full force.

"Cam." I moaned. My toes curled and my spine tingled.

"That's it, baby. Give me everything." He sped up his pace, pounding in and out of me harder.

With the force of his thrusts, he hit that spot inside of me to make another orgasm rip out of me like a volcano.

"Thank fuck." He groaned as he felt my pussy clenching his cock. And then he stilled.

I watched in avid fascination as his entire body strung tight and then like a flash, all of the muscles loosened.

Thank God Laci's room was on the other side of the house.

As my body slowly came back down from its high, I felt his arms wrap around me as he stood, taking me with him. His hands were under my ass while his cock was still buried deep inside of me.

My breath left my lungs as he slammed me against the wall. His mouth was on mine as his tongue danced with my own.

He started to move in and out of me yet again. I didn't know how I could cum so fast a second time, but here I was right there on the edge.

The moment one of his hands left my ass to play with my clit, my back bowed as my orgasm ripped from my body.

It wasn't long before he was coming with me.

My body felt like jelly as he walked us backward to the bed where he laid us down in a boneless heap.

With Cameron wrapped around my body, I breathed in and out trying to calm my racing heart.

What I did know was that if I didn't get him out of my house and soon, I would be regretting everything that would soon follow, and that was the last thing that I wanted.

Sometimes when I close my eyes, I can't see. I only see her.

Chapter 7

Cam

Having her in my arms again felt so fucking right. I never wanted to leave this bed nor her, ever again.

However, it was apparent that Michelle didn't feel the same as me. I knew that because she rolled out of bed, walked to her bathroom, pulled her robe off the back door, turned, then she grabbed my clothes off of the floor and tossed them at me.

"Time for you to go." There was no emotion in her tone. None.

"Seriously? You're going to kick me out? What the fuck?" I bit out angrily.

"Yea, Cameron. I'm kicking you out. If you want more, you can come back on my next day off but only after Laci goes to sleep." I heard every word she said, but what I was furious about was the fact that I just had my dick in her and she was still calling me Cameron. Not Cam.

Just as I was about to open my mouth, she tossed her hand up, "No. This is how this is going to work if it even works. You had my heart a long time ago and then you crushed it. Obliterated it. You don't like it, then there's the door, don't let it hit your ass on the way out."

And with that, I watched as she turned, walked to the bathroom, closed, and locked the door and moments later I heard her shower running.

Everything in me told me to stay right here and talk this out with her, to make her see that I have regretted that one night. To make her understand that her teary eyes when she ran out of the clubhouse that night seven years ago, still haunts me in my dreams.

However, given the blank tone she had tossed my way, I knew that it was a waste of time. Therefore, I was going to play this her way and prove to her that I was the man for not only her but for Laci as well.

Once I had my clothes on and pulled on my boots, I walked out of her house but not before I locked her door.

Operation Claim my Woman and Child is a go.

Grabbing my phone to see who had called me, I saw that it had been Powers. Mounting my bike I called him back.

"Finally you fucker." He said angrily.

"Was busy, man," I told him, fingering my gas tank that also had her name on it. I've been hers since the moment I took my first breath and I'll continue to be hers until I take my last.

I heard the skepticism in his tone, "You're never busy."

"When I finally have the woman of my dreams beneath me, Pres. nothing, not even you nor the club will pull me away." I told him honestly.

"Ahh. Got it. Church in the am."

Nodding, I said, "Right."

After a beat, he said, "Happy for you brother."

I chuckled darkly, "She fucking kicked me out."

With that statement, there was silence on the other end and then I heard him roaring with laughter, "Fucking love that woman."

Snarling, I hung up on him. Fucker.

Backing my bike out of her driveway, I looked up at the house in time to see her looking at me through the curtains in the living room. I pulled my hand up to cover it over my heart.

Then I watched in amazement as she did the same.

With that, I started up my bike and headed home. Home to a house that was her dream house. Everything in it had been done with thoughts of her.

Walking down the hall I stopped at one of the bedrooms, opening the door, I stood in the doorway as something came to mind.

Nodding my head, after church, my ass was headed to the store.

The next day I found myself grabbing a red cart as I headed to the home décor side of the store.

I knew what I looked like. I had my kutte on and was putting girly shit that was similar to what was in Laci's bedroom.

Having pink fucking furry pillows in my cart had gotten a lot of women staring at me. It wasn't condemnation, no it was admiration.

"Takes a big man that loves his daughter to do this." The cashier told me.

I nodded, not correcting her. "She deserves the best."

Arriving home, I started to unload everything when I heard the roar of motorcycles.

Leaning out of my truck it was to see Powers, Lil, Heathen, June, Greek, Melia, Lincoln, Savage, Zeke, and Skinner pulling up and parking their bikes in front of a black van.

No one said a word as they converged on the van, pulling out bags and buckets of paint.

"You sure about this?" Powers asked.

"Deadly. They're mine." I told him as I grabbed the bags from my truck.

"Proud to call you my brother." Skinner had said it so low that I had to strain to hear what he had said.

"Thanks, man." Emotion clogged my throat.

Four hours later with the help of my brothers, my family, we had Laci's room finished and the master closet redone.

Stepping back to inspect the room, I was amazed to see how similar it looked to her room. Hell, I even went and bought the shit for a tank. I didn't know what she had in the damn thing but the kit was there for her to set it up however she needed it.

"Fuck I'm starving," Heathen grumbled.

"Y'all want to hit that new restaurant in town?" June asked.

And that was how we all found ourselves thirty minutes later while we waited for the paint to dry.

"Well, damn, it's not often that I get men as hot as y'all in our restaurant." Smiles broke out.

It was Savage that said, "Well darlin' you give us great service and we will be back to give you our hotness."

The young waitress blushed like a June bride.

After we ate and had our stomachs full, we paid and made our way out of the restaurant but what happened next had my fists clenching at my sides.

Never make the same mistake twice unless he's hot.

Chapter 8

Michelle

The next day we had just walked out of a boutique when Laci looked over, then grabbed my hand and started to walk me in the direction that her eyes were trained on.

Looking up to see what had garnered that reaction was to see six motorcycles parked outside of a diner.

The moment we made it to the bikes I heard, "Yo, Michelle, Laci?" Looking near one of the bikes I smiled when I saw Lincoln.

"Lincoln, hey. How are you?" I smiled at him.

"Doing good. What are two beautiful ladies like y'all up to?" Lincoln was handsome, but he was no match for Cameron, sadly.

"Spending the rest of my day off shopping. The normal." I shrugged, thanks to covering for someone a week ago, I only had to work half a shift today.

"Michelle." I inhaled a breath as I looked over at Cameron.

"Cameron." I nodded then saw his face harden. I know I had called him Cam when we had been intimate, but he had a long way to go, didn't he?

"Hey, Cameron!" Laci said excitedly.

Lincoln raised a brow as he looked between us, "Uh, you two know each other?"

Cameron smirked, "Yeah you can say that."

"Their soul mates." I was starting to regret telling my daughter everything. Covering her mouth with my hand to stop what she was about to say next.

Cameron grinned full out, "She's right you know." Glaring at the butthead, I grabbed Laci's hand.

"It was good to see you, Lincoln. Have a good one." I turned away from them, taking Laci with me.

"Nothing for me? Even after last night?" I froze mid-step. Turned slowly as I gave him my eyes.

The moment his eyes locked with mine; I saw him flinch, "Yeah."

However, before anything else could be said, it was Laci that spoke, "Cameron, do you want to come to dinner tonight? Mommy is making homemade lasagna."

I gritted my teeth. A cocky smile hit his face as he looked down at my daughter with something in his eyes and I knew that I was in trouble. Deep trouble. It was love.

"One condition peanut." I saw a gleam in his eyes.

She placed the hand that wasn't in mine on her hip as she cocked it, "And that is?"

Chuckles from the others broke out as Cameron grinned, "You call me Cam and I'm there."

I knew what that meant. Everyone standing there knew what it meant.

"Okay, Cam. See you at six." She said as we both walked away from them.

Only not before I heard Lincoln ask, "That her?"

I waited with bated breath slowing down when I heard, "Yeah. That's her."

The moment we got home Laci walked in the house then stopped and turned, "Are you mad at me mommy?"

I crunched my brow, "For what sweet pea?"

"For inviting Cam to dinner without asking." She was twiddling her thumbs in nervousness.

Smiling, I knelt in front of her, "Livid." I tickled her belly as she giggled.

"No baby, I'm not mad. To be honest I like the fact that you like him. He's a good man to have in your corner should you ever need him."

"Like what Mommy?" She wrinkled her little brow.

"Can you keep a secret for me?" I asked

She nodded enthusiastically, "If something were to ever happen to me, your grandmother, or your aunt I'd ask Cameron to step in and raise you."

"Wow. You really did love him, didn't you mommy?"

"Yes, baby I really did."

"He asked me to call him Cam, why do you still call him Cameron?"

"Because a long time ago he took that away from me."

She growled as she asked, "Let me know if I need to kick him tonight." I smiled down at her as I tapped her on the nose.

"Sounds good baby. Go feed Sparks."

I had just set everything down on the counter while Laci watched a movie and started on the homemade pasta when there was a knock on the door.

Laci jumped up off the couch as she skipped to the door, "I got it."

"Check before you open the door sweet pea," I warned.

She called out in a sing-song voice at the door, "Who is it?"

"Your prince for the evening. It's Cam." Her giggle of laughter as she opened the door caused a smile to form on my face.

Damn, he looked good.

He had on dark wash jeans with his black motorcycle boots, a black button-up shirt with the sleeves rolled up to his elbows showing off his massive forearms. Of course, he had on his kutte.

"What have you got there?" It was then that I noticed the bouquet of wildflowers in his hand and something in a grocery bag in the other.

Damn, I'm a hoe. I didn't even notice those.

His eyes came to mine as he said, "Flowers for your mommy and this is for you." He told her as he looked down at her and handed her the bag.

She took it then looked at the flowers, "How did they not get messed up on the bike?"

"Put them in my saddlebags carefully." He winked.

I watched as she opened the bag while he stood there biting his bottom lip, he was nervous. I stifled the laugh that tried to come out. It was endearing.

Then I saw Laci freeze as she looked in the bag. Her eyes came to mine and I froze at the tears in her eyes.

Like a shot, she ran to Cameron and hugged him. He knelt down on the ground as he wrapped his arms around her and held her close.

Wiping my hands I walked over to them and took the bag from her grasp and then gasped.

Inside of the bag was something that we have been looking for but unable to find, two beanie babies, my girl fucking loved them, even though they were hard to find.

The ones he had found were the tie-dye beanie babies and the cotton candy pink teddy bear.

"Did I do good?" He asked as Laci still clung to him.

"Yes." She hiccupped through her tears.

"Good." I saw the nervousness leave him.

Grinning, I grabbed the flowers he held out to me, grabbed a vase from underneath the sink, filled it with water, and placed them inside of it, putting the vase in the middle of the island.

In that time, Laci had pulled Cameron to her bedroom and I was sure, had him put them with her collection on the top of her bookshelf so they wouldn't get messed up.

Grinning to myself, I finished the pasta and started it to cook. Then I grabbed the hamburger, seasoned it, and started it as well.

While that was cooking I chopped up some garlic and onions then added that to the pan as well.

"Need any help?" I looked up to see him standing in the open hallway beside the kitchen.

"Yeah, you can cut up the tomatoes, cucumbers, and onion for the salad." With that, he walked to the kitchen and color me surprised when he actually washed his hands.

Looking over his shoulder to see the smile on my face he tossed me a wink and said, "Sounds good."

Once he finished he made his way to me, moved my hair off of my shoulder, and placed a kiss on my neck.

I had grabbed everything and set it on one end of the island, when I asked, "Do you want a drink?"

"What have you got?" I grabbed the dish towel, wiped my hands, and then opened the fridge.

"Beer, sweet tea, lemonade, soda, chocolate milk, and water." I grabbed a beer for myself.

"Yeah, you're definitely a momma. Looks good on you. I'll have a beer." Grinning, I grabbed one for him then smiled as Laci came back in the main room and continued watching her movie.

Side by side we worked together. I didn't say anything about the times our shoulders had touched.

Once he was finished without a word to me, he grabbed his beer and walked into the living room, taking the floor right out from under me as he sat down beside Laci and watched a princess movie with her.

After everything was finished I popped the dish in the oven and set the timer for twenty-five minutes.

Walking into the living room I sat down beside Laci and finished watching the movie with her and Cameron.

"This smells great." He told me after he helped me carry everything to the table and I had to bite back a smile at remembering watching the two of them setting the table.

"My mommy can cook." Smiling at my little girl I winked at her.

I watched as Cameron got a forkful of lasagna and put it in his mouth. The things that mouth could do. I felt my cheeks heat, so trying to hide that fact I got my own bite.

When I looked up it was to see him staring at me with an all-knowing grin.

"Dickhead." I muttered.

He guffawed at me.

"Mommy, you shouldn't say bad words." I groaned.

Cameron gave me a wink. The asshat.

The rest of the meal was filled with questions from everyone and answers. Laughter followed.

"Y'all mind if I come over every night your mom cooks? Damn." He moaned as he rubbed his stomach.

Laci nodded as she ate the last of her salad. My girl was like me, she didn't waste food.

While I had been cleaning up the kitchen after telling Cameron that I had it all covered, he had been reading to Laci.

Grinning, I placed a kiss on her forehead as she snored softly.

Walking Cameron to the door I stopped on the porch when he said, "Thanks for having me over, I had a great time."

"Thanks for coming over. Umm, I'm off Wednesday night if you want to come over and have dinner with us. If not then that's cool too."

"Yeah, I'd like that," He told me as he stepped up to me.

The moment his warm calloused hand touched my cheek my eyes closed of their own accord.

His mouth was hot on mine as I leaned into the kiss. Our tongues continued to dance to a rhythm that only they knew.

We both pulled away, trying to get air back into our lungs.

"Have a good night Cam."

Then I watched as a breath-taking smile hit his face, "Fuck. Been dreaming of hearing my name from those lips for six long fucking years. Missed the fuck out of you babe. I'll see y'all Wednesday but I'll see you tomorrow night. Night baby."

What he didn't know was that after the first time we had fucked, well-made love really, was that he got under my skin. Yet again.

What really caused that to happen? Hearing him reading Laci a bedtime story. The six-foot-two biker laid on a cotton candy pink bed as he read *The Princess and The Dragon* to her until she fell asleep.

And for the life of me, I didn't care. I knew that the possibility of him hurting me again was high up on the list but I prayed with everything in me that it wouldn't be the case.

Something in his eyes when he left that night for the clubhouse told me that I didn't need to worry.

First God created man, then he had a better idea…

Chapter 9

Cam

"What movie do you want to watch tonight, peanut?" I was sitting in the living room with her while Michelle started dinner. I had tried to help her but had gotten shooed out of there.

"Can't. My teacher gave me this packet to see how far ahead I was with my class. I gotta work on it."

"Need any help?"

It was fucking adorable when she bit her bottom lip, "Yes, will you go over them after I do them to make sure I'm doing them right?"

Laci was six fucking years old and so far beyond her years, it was astounding.

Grinning, I nodded, "Yeah peanut."

I had just checked over her work, giving her a fist bump when I glanced up to see Michelle watching, "What?"

She jumped, almost as if she didn't realize she was watching us, "Nothing." Then she turned and finished.

We had just laid Laci down for the night and we were sitting on her front porch swing.

Taking a leap I asked, "Anything you want to know? Ask me anything, Michelle. I know you want to keep me at arm's reach, but baby, I want it all with you. I want you in my life in every way imaginable. I want Laci to call me dad if that's what she wants."

Waiting for her to reply was like telling a kid they had to wait for three hours to open presents on Christmas morning, "Truth?"

"Always." Fucking finally.

"Did you fuck Mina?" she asked with a slight tremor in her tone.

Fuck, this wasn't how I saw this conversation going. "No, I never fucked Mina. She wanted it, but I never fucked her."

"Did you do anything with her?" I knew that she disliked Mina, I knew why and I could only imagine that what I had done had made that betrayal that much harder on her.

Lifting my head to look at her I locked eyes with her as I said, "No. She wasn't you."

"And yet you believed her over me…." There was where we stalled with every single fucking conversation.

Dropping my head I placed my hands on the back of my neck. What more could I fucking do here? "I realized my mistake the moment I pulled up the photo after you ran out and saw all of the earrings in the other woman's ear."

"Cameron, I just… I don't know." Fuck but I hated that name coming out of her mouth. I wanted us back to when she called me Cam. Knew it was going to be hard as fuck to get us back to that, but I didn't think that it was going to be this fucking hard.

"Just remember the good times we had before that night. Remember how we were with each other. Sometimes people wait a lifetime for a connection like the one we shared. I found my person at sixteen years old."

In a whisper, she said, "And yet you threw that connection away like it was nothing more than garbage."

"Didn't hear you deny the connection."

"No, what that was, was puppy love, Cameron. I grew up and realized that connections like ours aren't meant to be forever."

"Tell me how you really feel," I said sarcastically.

"You told me that when we started this that you wanted honesty and nothing else. What did you expect?"

"Well, I was hoping that after everything I have done to show you that I'm not the same man I was seven years ago you would forgive me for what happened back then."

"Cameron, you didn't just break my heart, you crushed it. No one has ever hurt me like you did."

"So you're going to lump me in the same boat as that piece of filth." I knew that she could feel the fury rolling off me in waves.

"No. What that man did to me, although he stole from me, he did give me my greatest gift in life. I couldn't have wished for a better daughter even if I had molded her myself. But what you did, you hurt the one thing that should have been handled with the gentlest care. Something that would never heal because you crushed it into a million pieces."

"I've done everything I can think of to show you I'm not the same fucking punk-ass kid I was back then." I stood angrily, running my hands over my hair, "Fuck."

My temper was about to boil over and before I said something I would no doubt regret I growled, uncaring who heard I said to her, "When you're ready to get off your goddamn high horse. Call me." And with that, I walked away.

Sitting at the clubhouse I was trying to calm the fuck down and figure out if I was just wasting my damn time or to keep trying.

***

The next day, I had been hoping but not expecting her to call, so when my hand was in a transmission, my phone rang, I grabbed it and checked the screen.

Seeing it was her I answered, "Hey."

"Hey, look, I umm…" She didn't say anything which caused my temper to flare yet a-fucking-gain, no one got to me like she did.

"Spit it out, Michelle. I'm busy."

"Can you come over after she goes to sleep tonight?"

"Yeah." Then I hung up the phone.

Just as I put my phone in my back pocket, Greek walked over to me.

"Hey man, I have a few prospects I need you to look over," Greek told me as he handed me a file folder.

Sighing, I grabbed the red rag I had hanging from my back pocket, wiped my hands off, and then I tagged the folder.

Looking over them, all but one were okay with me. "This one. Something doesn't sit right with me."

I handed him the paper as he looked at it. Saw what I saw and said, "Gotcha. The rest we can take to church tonight."

"10-4." After I finished rebuilding the transmission, I cleaned up then grabbed one of the subs the club whores made.

After I ate, Powers called out, "Church."

Tossing my trash away, I walked to the table, put my phone in the box outside of church, then walked in and took my seat.

Within minutes everyone was sitting down and the door was closed.

Powers banged the gavel then gave the floor to Greek.

"Here are the candidates for prospects. Cam already said no to one of them, but these are up for consideration." Greek said as he handed the folder to Powers.

"What was it with the one you said no to that got your attention?"

"Woman filed a restraining order on him."

"Got it." We didn't give two shits if someone had a criminal record. Didn't matter to us if you murdered a rapist. Didn't matter to us if you took out a pedophile. What did matter to us was if you had a record of harming a woman. That wasn't just a no, but a hell fucking no.

You want to put your hands on a woman? You'll deal with us. Period.

After all the brothers looked at the other applicants, they voiced their opinions. All of them were a go.

"We will do the official vote tomorrow night. Anything anyone needs to bring to the table?"

When no one said a word, he banged the gavel and we all stood.

I grabbed a shot that Melia had poured for us, pounded it on the bar stop as was our ritual, and downed it.

Just as I was getting ready to leave Savage walked over to us and said, "Talked to the one we said no to. He was waiting out in the clubhouse. Think we need to hear him out."

Sighing, I glanced at my watch. Laci went to bed in thirty minutes.

"Got somewhere you need to be?" Powers asked.

"Laci goes to sleep in thirty. Heading over to have a talk with Michelle."

"Tell the man to make it fucking quick," Powers told Savage.

The moment Savage returned with the man; I didn't see him hurting a woman. You could tell. It was their eyes that gave them away and this man, no, all he had in them was pain.

He was tall like the rest of us, but he wasn't as bulky as us. Man needed to put some meat on his bones.

"Look, I know I have a restraining order against me. I didn't try to hide that fact. The only reason I have it is because I have a daughter that the bitch refuses to let me see."

None of us batted an eye at the term bitch either. What we did do though was growl that the woman refused to let him see.

"Here are the court documents that I have tried to file numerous times, but it doesn't help that her daddy is a fucking judge and her brother is a fucking lawyer."

We all looked over the documents and then I said, "You make the cut. We will help you get your daughter." I told him as I slapped his back then looked at Powers and nodded my approval of the man.

With that, Powers said, "We will vote tomorrow."

"I'm out. Call if you need me." I tossed over my shoulder.

Smirking Powers said, "Right."

Flipping him off, I walked out of the clubhouse and to my bike.

On the way over to her house, I replayed over and over in my mind what I was going to say to her.

Shutting my bike off at the end of her drive I walked it up and parked it next to her truck.

Before I could knock she opened the door. Fucking hell what she had on? Seeing her standing there in one of my old t-shirts and nothing else from what I could see?

I said fuck the conversation I was having with her. It could fucking wait. My dick, however, could not.

Rushing her I slammed my mouth down on hers. Pushing her into the house, I kicked the door closed, leaned down, wrapped my hands around her panty-covered ass, and lifted.

Her legs wrapped around my waist and held on. Our mouths never separated.

The moment we made it to her room, I did the same thing to her bedroom door.

Letting go of her she lowered her feet to the floor and within a second we were tearing our clothes off in a frenzy.

Never have I allowed my kutte to be thrown on the floor but right then, I didn't give a single fuck.

Nor did I give a single fuck when we were both naked and she dropped to her knees in front of me.

Throwing my hand out to brace it on the wall at her back I dropped my head when her tongue circled around the tip of my cock.

The moment she pulled my cock inside of her mouth I moaned. "Goddamn baby."

She fucking giggled.

The moment my cock hit the back of her throat, she vibrated around it, I almost came right then and there. "Fuck sweetheart."

Wrapping my hand around her braid I held her head still while I pumped in and out of her.

Noticing that she had a gag reflex yet it didn't seem to bother her…shit.

When her hand came up to cup my balls I told her through gritted teeth, "You don't want me to come in your mouth, you better pull back."

Her response? That was to let go of my balls and grab the backs of my thighs to keep me right where I was.

Within seconds my cum was shooting out of my dick and I roared.

After I came, I pulled out it was to see her licking her lips, bending down I wrapped my arms around her, lifted, then spun and tossed her on the bed.

The moment I climbed on top of her, I moved my dick along her folds. Feeling her wetness I didn't hesitate to slam inside of her.

It was only when I did that, I realized that I didn't have a condom on. I stilled.

As if she sensed what was going on she lifted up and when her mouth was scant seconds away from mine, she muttered the magic words, "I'm on birth control."

Crossing the distance, I kissed her hard. I kept pumping into her hard and fast. Grabbing her legs I tossed them over one shoulder and then drove even deeper inside of her.

I felt my eyes fucking cross.

The moment I dropped a finger to her clit and flicked it, her back arched.

"Cam…" She moaned

"Come on baby. Give it to me."

And that was what she did when I felt her pussy clench all around me signaling the release of her orgasm.

"It just gets better and better." She said as I came, filling her up with my cum.

As I pulled my dick out of her tight pussy, I watched her eyes. There was something in them that I couldn't fully decipher but I knew that I was wearing her down.

"Never doing you with a condom ever again. Son of a bitch."

Life Status: currently holding it all together with one bobby pin.

Chapter 10

Michelle

Did I like that I was nothing more than a booty call? That didn't bother me. Did it bother me that he only came over at night after my daughter had gone to sleep? Again, no.

I was the one to make that play. Sure when that animal had raped me, it had burned something deep inside of me. It had taken away my innocence that wasn't his.

However, all of that aside, what Cameron Bryant did to me, in my opinion, was much worse. Only I had been holding onto that hatred for too long. It was high time I let it go and stopped being a bitch to the man that still held my crushed heart in his fists. I never really got it back, maybe just maybe he would weld the pieces back together.

At least I did get to have my body under, on top of, beside of, the hottest man I had ever seen.

He had just rolled over off of me and laid down on his back, both of us were inhaling some much-needed air.

My skin was sweaty and sticky.

"Don't make me leave Michelle. Please. Don't make me leave." My heart ripped wide fucking open at his words and his tone. It had to have come from the deepest part of him.

That was my wake-up call.

Looking over at him to see him staring up at the ceiling, I rolled, ignoring my body's protest, and placed my head on his chest. Throwing caution to the wind and doing the same thing I have told Laci to do, look for the good no matter what, therefore I whispered, "Stay."

As soon as those words left my mouth, he rolled us until his arm was under my pillow and I was wrapped in his embrace, with a kiss on my bare shoulder he said, "Thank you."

I shivered at the sincerity in his tone. This man was my undoing. Irrevocably so.

We both climbed out of bed and cleaned up. I wasn't a fan of sleeping with cum leaking out of me. Ick.

The moment we were both cleaned up I pulled his t-shirt back on and replaced my panties then climbed into bed.

"Like that, you had something of mine all this time." I smiled, leaned in, and kissed his bearded jaw.

He wrapped me in his arms and pulled the covers over the both of us.

Sighing in his arms I closed my eyes as I heard, "Good night baby."

What I didn't know was that halfway through the night Cam had gotten up, checked the house, and checked on Laci before he climbed back in bed with me.

The moment I stepped into the kitchen the next morning I saw Laci looking out of the front window.

"Morning baby, how'd you sleep?"

"Okay. Why are there boots at the front door?" Laci asked sleepily.

Before I could reply to her, Cam came walking out of my bedroom in his jeans and nothing else. My eyes traveled along his chest.

"Mom. Your heartbeat doing that thing again?" Laci asked in with a snicker.

Tapping her nose I winked at her. "Hush."

"Good morning, beautiful." What I wouldn't give to hear that every morning, but things we want the most, normally never happen. But I had a feeling that it was going to happen. Happiness felt so good again.

It was then that I felt his finger underneath my chin as he lifted my face to his, "What's that smile for?"

"Nothing. Just happy."

"Me too baby. Me fucking too." He placed a soft kiss on my lips then walked over to Laci.

Wrapping an arm around her shoulders he said, "Morning peanut."

"Morning Cam."

After I made a quick breakfast of bacon and eggs I got ready for my shift at the hospital while Laci got ready for school.

Walking into the kitchen after getting my hair tamed it was to see Cam stuffing things into Laci's lunch box. I froze.

"You okay?" He asked, seeing the look on my face.

"Yes, just nice to have help." He winked, not saying a word as he handed Laci her lunch box.

After we were all ready we walked out the front door.

While I locked up Cam took Laci to my truck and helped her climb in.

After he did that he rounded my truck and opened my door for me. "Have a good day at work baby, I'll bring lunch."

"Sounds good. Thanks for staying Cam." Then I took that leap of faith. "If you're free for dinner tonight, maybe bring a change of clothes."

"Nothing could keep me away baby. I'll be over after church." With a soft kiss, he closed the door and headed for his bike.

***

Smiling as Laci kept looking out of the back window, Cam followed us to school.

Just as I had dropped Laci off at school I had a call from the hospital. Sighing, I answered the call, "Hello?"

"Ms. O'Connell there was a pile-up on the interstate. How far from the hospital are you?"

Sighing, knowing I wouldn't be able to grab myself my normal coffee, "Ten minutes. Have Mackenzie ready a coffee for me please."

"Good. Please hurry." Lisa stated then hung up on me.

Cam had just turned off the main road to head to the clubhouse, I grinned.

What I didn't know was that two days from now the happiness I had been feeling was going to be interrupted and everything I thought I knew would change.

If you can't laugh at your own problems, call me and I'll laugh at them.

Chapter 11

Cam

I had just parked my bike to eat lunch with Michelle when I noticed the activity in the hospital.

Walking inside with the bag in my hand I looked to the nurse's station to see her head hanging down.

Walking over to her, placing my hand on her lower back I asked, "Hey, everything okay?"

"Yeah, there was a pile-up on the interstate and there were mass casualties, they need me to stay but I can't get a hold of anyone to pick up Laci from school."

"Need me to go and get her?" Please say yes. Fuck. Please.

She bit her bottom lip as she considered it. "You understand what this will mean right?"

"Yeah, darlin' I know that I will be with your greatest treasure in life. I won't allow anything to hurt her."

"Yes but that's not it. You ever hurt me again, means you hurt her. And if that ever happens Cameron Bryant, you'll never see either one of us again." The moment I saw one of the tears she had been holding back fall, I wiped them away with my thumb.

"Honey, nothing in this world comes before you and that little girl. I'll kill myself before I ever allow anything that has to do with me harm y'all. You need me to leave the club to make that happen than say the word. You want me to wear a chastity belt and you hold the key? Again, just say the word."

"Okay, Cam." Closing my eyes at hearing my name finally come from her lips. Fucking perfection.

Placing a kiss on her forehead I murmured, "What school?"

"Elwood Primary. I'll call them and let them know that you can check her out." She was pulling out her phone to do just that.

"Okay, babe. I'll text you and let you know when I get her and where we go. Gotta run home and swap out my bike for my truck." Leaning forward I placed a kiss on her temple.

"Here's lunch, make sure you eat," I told her sternly.

Watching her face soften was enough for me to miss out on what I had grabbed for us to eat.

"Thanks, honey." She murmured softly.

Tossing her a wink I walked out of the hospital smiling the entire fucking way.

The moment I parked my bike at my house and then got in my truck I headed for the school.

Elwood Primary was the same school that a few of the kids in the MC were either attending or had been attending. They ought to be used to seeing men with kuttes, however, the old bat in the office wasn't.

As soon as I hit the button to be let in, I opened the door and walked into the main office. A woman sitting behind the counter sneered at me, that was nothing new. "Sorry but gang affiliate things aren't allowed on school property."

"He isn't in a gang; he is a motorcycle enthusiast." Hearing Laci stick up for me melted my heart as she rounded the counter.

The moment she made it to my side the woman asked, "Your name?"

"Cameron Bryant. Picking up Laci. Her mother called ahead."

Her next statement caused my fists to clench. "I'll just call and make sure it's okay for you to take her."

Growling I tamped down my anger, I wouldn't show that side of me in front of Laci, "You can do that but she's elbow deep in trying to save lives due to a mass pile-up on the interstate. And lady, you're sure not setting a good example for students treating people like you are."

"What Cam said. You need to go back to kindergarten and learn some manners." Did I attempt to cover Laci's mouth? That would be a negative.

Chuckling I said "Hey there peanut. Ready to roll?"

"Yep. What happened?" She asked as I grabbed her Care Bear backpack and slung it over my shoulder.

"Accident on the interstate, your mom had to stay."

"Gotcha." Walking out of the school with her little hand in mine I held the truck door open for her. The moment she climbed inside I closed it, then rounded the front of the truck to get inside.

As soon as I started the truck up I asked, "Hungry?"

"Yes! School lunch wasn't that good today." I nodded knowingly.

"What are you in the mood for?"

I watched her face in the rear-view mirror as she grinned and said, "Pizza!"

"Girl after my own heart." Smiling, I turned on some rock. And shit you not, Laci started to sing with every single song on the radio. So here we were, the windows down sitting at a red light while we cranked out rock songs and played air guitar.

I've been kicking my own ass these past years, but no more than I am right at this moment. I should have been there for Michelle. Should've stepped in and helped her raise Laci. Had I known she was pregnant, I wouldn't have stopped trying to find her. I would've camped out in front of her mother's house and waited for her mother to come to terms that I wasn't going anywhere.

But had that happened, I was sure that she wouldn't be as fucking awesome as she is now. Michelle had raised Laci with love, and there was no better way.

We had just walked into the best pizza parlor in town when the hostess asked, "How many?"

Ignoring the sultry look she was giving me I said, "Two."

"Love daddy-daughter dates." The hostess whose name tag read Holy stated.

I didn't bother to correct her and when I looked down at Laci I saw her staring at me with a confused brow. "What?"

"Nothing. I like it." And that was the end of it. No more was said as we were seated and I ordered a Dr. Pepper for me, a Lemonade for Laci, and a large pizza with everything on it.

However, my good mood ended when I heard that voice. The voice, six years later and it still caused my anger to boil, asked, "I didn't know you had a daughter."

"I don't. She's a friend's daughter." Knew the moment the words came out of my mouth that I shouldn't have said a goddamn thing. Should've ignored her and carried on with my dinner date with Laci.

"Well then, mind if I join y'all." She said in a voice that grated on my last nerve.

However, before I could tell the woman not no, but fuck no, Laci spoke up in her cute little voice and I fell head over heels for her, "Yes we do mind."

"Your mother obviously never taught you any manners." Mina snarled.

My entire body stilled. "Mina…"

"Wait your Mina? You're the evil woman that showed Cam some bull crap pictures and caused him to dump my mom. She was right, you are a nasty piece of work."

Mina stared down at Laci, and Laci, being her mother's daughter, said, "Leave already. Trash like you isn't wanted."

It took everything in me to not burst out laughing.

We both watched as Mina stormed out of the restaurant, only when she left did I turn to look at Laci.

Leaning into the table, she whispered, "Do me a favor?"

"Name it."

"Don't tell my mom I said a bad word."

I held in the laugh that wanted to bubble up, if she heard the way we talk at the clubhouse, I was sure Laci would be the one grilling me for the language.

So that being the case, I did the only thing that would stop the laughter from coming out, I did what any grown-ass man would do. I lifted my right hand and held out my pinky to her, "Pinky promise."

Her little finger wrapped around mine and that was that.

Laci and I had made dinner and it was the shocked expression on Michelle's face that had caused me to throw my head back and laugh. Sure it was nothing like what she cooked, but still, who went wrong with blueberry pancakes and bacon for dinner?

Later that night after Laci fell asleep, I sat on one of Michelle's loungers while I sipped on a soda. My woman was a single mom through and through.

"What do you need to get your doctorate?" I asked her.

With her leg thrown over mine, she said, "Someone to watch Laci and get her after school. The classes are vigorous."

"You got me and the whole club babe," I told her.

It was a long few minutes before she responded, "Do I have you."

"Told you, baby, all you gotta do is to say I'm your man." Smirking, I tossed her wink.

"Might take you up on that." She murmured as she took a pull from her own soda

Just as I was about to respond to her, she jumped up and whirled, "Mommy, my tummy hurts."

Laci stood there in her little pink nightgown while holding onto a plush dragon as she wiped at her eye sleepily.

"I'm sorry baby, let's go get you some ginger ale and see if we can get it to stop hurting." Without a backward glance, she led Laci into the house and closed the sliding glass door.

Did it bother me that she didn't say a word to me, yes in a way, but I knew that Laci always came first. No matter what. I wouldn't have it any other way.

The next day after I had finished on a build I drove to the hospital to check on with Michelle on Laci. I had been worried about Laci all morning. I sent her a text but never got anything back and I called her, twice.

Walking into the hospital I headed straight for Michelle. "How's Laci?"

She jumped, then answered me, "Stomach bug I think. It's going around her school."

"Does she need anything?" I asked.

"No. My mom has her today. But thank you, Cam, that means a lot." Smiling down at her I put a strand of her hair that had fallen out of her ponytail behind her ear.

"Sorry I couldn't answer your call, it's been a madhouse here." It was then that the nurse Mackenzie handed her a tablet.

Leaning forward I placed a kiss on her forehead then smiled, "Go, kick-ass baby, I'll see y'all tonight."

Giving me a wink she turned on her heel and walked back into a patient's room.

Sitting at the clubhouse with a warm beer sitting in front of me after we voted on the new prospects, all of them getting the approval, I tried to come up with a plan. A plan to move us forward. I was ready to put a ring on her finger and to give her my last name. Hell, the ring had been sitting in my safe at my house for four fucking years.

Told myself when I saw it, that the moment she came back to town, if she were to give me the time of day, I'd drop to my knees and ask her to be my wife.

Snapping me out of my thoughts it was Heathen that asked, "How are things?"

"Fuck one-minute things are great and the next, fuck man I just don't know."

"Keep trying Cam," Heathen said as he reached under the bar top and handed me a cold beer. "A woman scorned is hard to forgive." He was right about that, "The look she has for you. See it in June." And with that, he turned and walked away.

Grabbing the beer I took a swig of it. Processing everything that had gone down over the past couple of weeks.

But all of my thoughts stopped in their tracks when a call came over the scanner we had in the main room of the clubhouse.

Nothing really registered at first about the call, that was until the address that I had been going to almost every night after a certain little raven-haired beauty went to sleep.

I was up and off my stool so fast as I sprinted out of the clubhouse and to my truck.

On the way there my phone rang, "Michelle."

She was coughing and wheezing, "Cam…"

"I'm on my way, baby. Be there in five." The rumbles of the motorcycles and the roar of Heathen's truck sounded behind me.

The moment I got there her entire house was on fire.

"What the fuck?" I asked no one in particular.

The rumble of bikes shut off as they all climbed off and took in the scene, but I paid them no mind. My eyes immediately scanned the area and when I saw my two girls, I all but ran over there to them.

The moment they saw me, they launched themselves in my arms while the paramedics scrambled after them trying to keep the oxygen masks over their noses.

"I've got you both. I'm right here." I soothed them both.

Two hours later after the fire was put out, I said, "Come on baby, y'all are staying with me." I told her in a tone that normally brooked no room for argument, however, that was not the case with Michelle. Hard-headed woman.

"No, Cam." She cried into my kutte. Both of my girls had my t-shirt underneath my kutte drenched, but I didn't give a damn.

"At least for a few nights honey. Laci looks dead on her feet." Sure that was a cheap shot, but the moment I saw the fight leak out of her, I knew.

She took in how tired Laci looked, I knew that moment she gave in, sighing, she muttered, "Okay."

Loading them up in my truck, I finished helping Heathen and Skinner as they loaded the only thing that was standing in her house. A fucking fireproof safe. Thank God the metal wasn't hot anymore.

They should put prizes in your Tampax box.

Your period sucks, but here's a 50% off ice cream coupon, you cranky bitch.

Chapter 12

Michelle

Walking numbly into Cam's house, nothing registered.

It didn't register when Cam first led me to his bathroom, started the shower, and showed me where everything was.

Neither did it register that he had taken Laci to another part of his house.

When I felt his warm body wrap around mine in the shower, I turned, buried my face into his neck, and cried.

He didn't move, he just let the warm water run over both of us.

When I had cried everything out, he let go of me then grabbed the shampoo bottle that was just like the one I had at home, in fact, everything in this shower were exact replicas of what I had in my show… my nonexistent shower.

He washed my hair and conditioned it. After he rinsed it all out of my hair, he soaped up a loofa and then washed my body.

After I was rinsed off I kissed him softly on the lips then stepped from the shower. Grabbed two towels and I sighed in blissful warmth when I realized they were heated.

After I toweled off I grabbed one of his shirts that he had laying on the bathroom counter then walked to his bed.

He came out moments later with a comb in his hand. What shocked me was that he sat behind me and combed out the tangles in my hair.

After he finished, neither one of us said a word, it wasn't until Laci walked in the room and climbed on the bed that the silence was broken.

Sleepily she snuggled into my arms. I didn't bother to ask where her nightgown had come from.

Laying curled up in Cam's bed with Laci snoring softly in my arms, Cam climbed on the bed and surrounded us both, "Baby, it's going to be okay." He whispered into my hair.

And that was the last thing I remembered before joining Laci in a peaceful slumber.

Cam had lain awake all night making sure there were no threats.

That morning as I roused awake to find myself in bed alone, I rolled over and stretched.

Knowing that I was supposed to work today I looked over at the nightstand to see my phone plugged up to a charger.

Grabbing it I called Lisa, she was the Director of Emergency Medicine in the emergency room.

"Hello?"

"Hey Lisa, it's Michelle. I'm afraid I need someone to cover for me for a few days…" I started to say.

"Honey I know. I'm so sorry. I tried to call you last night to check on you and Laci but you didn't answer."

"Thank you. We got out of there in time. It was scary, that was for sure."

"Dr. Peters, Dr. Morelli, and Dr. Stone have already added their names on the schedule to cover your shifts for however long you need."

"Thank you, Lisa, and please tell them all thank you for me."

"You got it. You need us, you just say the word."

My eyes finally started to take in everything that was in Cam's bedroom and my breath caught.

What the hell? Everything was something that I would have picked out.

Remembering last night I jumped out of bed and went into the bathroom; it was the same. Down to the heated tiled floor.

I walked to his closet and again I froze. Staring dumbfounded at a few clothes that were hanging on the right side of his closet with tags on them. They were things I would have picked out.

In wonder, I pulled a day dress off of a hanger.

Then I walked to the bed and saw that my bra and panties from last night had been washed.

Pulling everything on I exited out of the bedroom to take in his house, and to look for the two of them.

Finding them in the massive kitchen, I stopped. He had black appliances, granite countertops, and an island. They were all top of the line, but that wasn't what really caught my attention when my eyes scanned over the open floor plan.

No, what caught my attention was the picture that was hanging above the white brick fireplace. It was of us on the night he had first bought his bike, it was in black and white. I had that picture still on my phone. Thank God.

"Morning beautiful. Sleep okay?" At Cam's voice, I turned my head to look at him.

"Yes, I did. Thank you for last night. Umm… mind explaining this house to me?"

He lifted his cup of what I assumed was coffee and said, "I think you know."

"Mommy, come look." Laci bounded out of her chair, ran to me, grabbed my hand, and pulled me down the hall. To say I was speechless was an understatement.

Her room. My God.

Walking in it was almost an exact replica of the one we had at our home. "I got a princess bed, and look." She continued to show me everything that was in her room.

Lifting my head it was to see Cam standing in the doorway with his arms crossed, "When did you do all of this?"

He walked into the room then leaned to whisper in my ear so only I would hear, "The day after you kicked me out of bed." Tears sprang in my eyes as I leaned my head into his chest.

His arms came around me as I whispered, "I'm so sorry Cam."

"No need to be sorry baby. You were protecting yourself and Laci. Had you not done that, I wouldn't have respected you at all."

After we ate he checked his phone then nodded, looking at me he said, "I know you don't want to but we need to head to the clubhouse. We gotta figure out how your house caught fire and the other ole' ladies are dying to meet you."

Knowing that having Cam in my life meant having them in my life. So I nodded.

The moment he shut the truck off, my eyes avoided that spot which Cam didn't miss.

He leaned over the console to whisper in my ear so Laci wouldn't hear, "I'll replace that memory baby. Make it better. Promise you, it'll be a different experience and one where I intend to make your toes curl."

Nodding, I kept my eyes focused on anything that wasn't that spot. He jumped out of his truck as I climbed out and got Laci down. We walked hand in hand while Laci held onto his other hand into the clubhouse.

The place hadn't changed much, they just had more tables and chairs along with some new artwork on the walls.

He walked us over to where a group of women were sitting. The moment they saw us, they stood.

"Ladies, this is my woman and my girl. Michelle and Laci. Baby, this is Lil, Power's ole' lady, Melia, Greek's ole' lady, and you already know June."

I offered each of them my hand, "Nice to meet y'all."

Then I heard a voice that belonged to Nathan, as he ran over and asked, "Hey Laci, want to come color?"

Without waiting for me to say a word, my girl let go of Cam's hand and then she followed them.

Grinning, I sat down in the chair Cam pulled out for me. Tipping my head back to look at him he leaned in, "Got Church baby. Be out in a minute. You need me, don't hesitate. Just knock on the door first okay?"

"Yeah, Cam." Grinning, he placed a kiss on my forehead then headed to the room I knew was called church.

Just as the door closed I looked up to see my mom walk in the clubhouse as she made a beeline for me, wrapping me in her arms.

"Grammie!" Laci said as she rushed over and hugged her.

For the next fifteen minutes, Laci told my mother about Cam's house and her room.

"How are you being so calm about this? Everything you owned was just burnt to a crisp." The woman who had been introduced as Lil asked me.

"I wouldn't be so calm had I not had that safe. Always being prepared, worked well for me. Had I lost Laci's baby things then yes, that would have me in tears, and I'd be a raging bitch."

"Well, I guess that is the bright side." June told me as she brought out a piece of paper, "Now, what are y'all's sizes and things."

"June, appreciate it, but no." I shook my head at her.

"Don't argue with her baby. This is what the club does. You know this." I bit my tongue at my mother's censuring tone.

"Had I not been forced to come here today; I never would've stepped foot on this property again," I whispered.

Just walking by the spot where my rape took place had tears in my eyes. I hadn't noticed that everyone had been watching me silently, not until I felt his presence at my back.

"Darlin, let's get Laci and take a drive." Nodding gratefully I stood, hugged my mother, then grabbed Laci's hand as we followed Cam out to his truck.

June

"What's her problem with the club? I mean her dad was a member, if I recall from the stories I had heard, she had been coming here a lot when she was younger."

I couldn't read Lil's expression as she said softly, "You know about the girl that was raped outside of the clubhouse in the parking lot seven years ago?"

"Yes. Everyone knows about that. It was a sad tragedy and a huge slap in the face for what Wrath MC stands for." I told her.

Then the floor was ripped right out from under me with what she said next, "That woman was Michelle."

I felt the mistrust that I got from Michelle clear out as I stared at Lil in horror. "Are you serious?"

"Deadly. She was dating Cam. He ended things with her because of bitch face Mina told him lies about her and instead of trusting Michelle, he trusted Mina. Long story short, he ended things with her. She ran out of here crying, a man was waiting in the shadows for an unsuspecting woman."

"Fucking asshole. Any clue where he is? I feel a little payback is coming his way." I snarled.

Lil smiled darkly then whispered, "No. He's six feet under. That was Cam's first kill."

I then made it my mission to support Michelle in any way I possibly could.

***

Michelle

"Where are we going?" I asked him as he pulled off the main highway and into the mall parking lot.

"You and Laci need shit babe."

"Cam, you don't have to do this," I told him.

He looked over at me and sighed, "Babe, whether you're ready to admit it or not, y'all are mine. Y'all have been mine for a very long time."

"But still, it wasn't your fault that our house caught fire, Cam."

"Be that as it may, don't give a fuck whose fault it was. I'll say this again, y'all are mine to take care of. Now let's go shopping."

"Cam, I don't like clothes from the mall, they are overpriced and stupid. We shop at Target." I told him.

With that, he nodded then pulled out of the parking lot and headed to Target.

***

"This is too much already." I sighed as I looked at the half-filled cart already. He had told Laci to get whatever her heart desired. And without a word to me, she did just that.

"Babe, I've got plenty of money. Buy what y'all need."

"Cam…"

"Fuck your so goddamn stubborn. Let me break this down for you yeah? Ever since I was fifteen I've been working. Busting my ass. I own my home outright. Bought it at nineteen. Own my truck, paid cash, same for my bike. For the past six years, I've bought what I needed and paid bills. Make plenty working in the garage doing custom bike builds, those fuckers are not cheap. Get my take from the club. Got over six figures just sitting in the bank."

Whispering, shocked at his words I said, "Okay."

After we had Cam's truck loaded down with the things we needed I turned to Laci and said, "Let's go get

Sparks." I was thanking my lucky stars that Sparks had a floppy tail as they called it and we had dropped him off with the vet's office to have his tail removed the day prior.

"Okay, mommy. Thank you Cam for having a tank ready."

"Welcome peanut."

After we got Sparks from the vet's office and paid, we headed back to Cam's. To say I was still shocked that he had built the house just like I wanted it to be an understatement.

Walking in through the doors in the light of day was an all too different experience. Seeing everything was such a shock to my system.

***

Cam

Five hours earlier at the clubhouse

The moment the doors were closed Powers banged the gavel. "What the fuck happened?" He roared.

"The fire was started at the back of the house. Fucking gasoline was poured on her back porch." Lincoln stated darkly.

Greek had the look of murder on his face, "Got the footage from a nearby house."

We all turned to watch and I felt the blood in my veins freeze. Seeing a woman that didn't bother to hide her face.

Before I could say her name, it was Skinner that mumbled, "Fucking bitch."

"Mina," Zeke said with a growl.

"Find the cunt. Bring her to the shed."

"Done," Gage said murderously. The rest of the men nodded their heads as well.

My hands started to itch to meet out my own brand of vengeance.

"Cam, go home to your ole' lady and your girl. The moment we have her, I'll call." I nodded to Powers then walked out of church only to hear Michelle's statement and to see all eyes on her, my fucking heart broke for her.

If it weren't for the fact that they needed me, I would've been out on the hunt too.

***

Michelle

I woke up to something moving softly over my curves, "Cam?"

"Yeah, baby. Gotta get to the clubhouse." I opened my tired eyes as I looked up at him. What I saw in those eyes caused shivers to run along my body.

"Everything okay?" I asked him, coming fully awake now.

"Yeah, baby. Be back to take Laci to school and you to work." I know that he didn't like that I wasn't taking more time off from work but he knew me. He knew that I hated being idle.

I worried my lower lip as I said, "Okay. Be careful."

I knew not to ask what happened within the club. I grew up in the club. I wasn't an ole' lady so I wasn't privy to anything.

What I didn't know was that I had said something in my sleep, and I hadn't heard his reply.

Until then, mio dolce amor, a thousand kisses; but give me none in return,

for they set my blood on fire

Chapter 13

Cam

Hearing Michelle say I love you was something else I had been dreaming about day and night.

Saying I love you back, was something that I didn't hide. Not from anyone.

The moment I pulled up to the clubhouse, I shut my bike off.

Then I let my temper run rampant through my veins.

Walking around the clubhouse to the back shed I saw four of my brothers nod at me.

Nodding back I walked into the shed to see the bitch with her arms tied above her head to a steel beam.

Now I didn't hurt women. Never. But what I would hurt was a piece of trash.

Without missing a beat and not saying a word to anyone I rushed her, then put all of my two hundred and twenty pounds into one solid punch to her face.

"That was for Michelle." Then I whipped my knife out from the small of my back and drove it straight through her stomach. "That was for Laci, you goddamn piece of shit." I roared at her.

Her body went limp.

No that just wouldn't do. I walked to the side of the building, turned the water on, and then I grabbed the hose and sprayed her in the face. Not stopping until she came to, spitting and sputtering trying not to inhale the water.

"Why?" I asked as I stopped with the hose.

Crying she muttered, "You were supposed to be mine."

"Wrong," Skinner said from behind me.

It was then that Lincoln came up to my side with a led pipe, stepped to her side, and slammed it into her left knee cap.

Then Zeke did the same to her right knee cap. Her howls of pain were music to my ears.

That was when Heathen stepped up, then no joke grabbed a hammer, and swung up into her vagina.

No one cringed. She didn't deserve the sentiment.

Skinner stepped up then without a word, he took two knives and sliced them down her face.

Powers was the last one left; all he did which was all that was needed was to spit in her face.

Wanting this person gone from this earth who was just a waste of space I pulled my nine-mil out of my shoulder holster, smiling darkly when her eyes widened.

"No. Please. No."

"Shouldn't have tried to kill my ole' lady and my daughter."

Leaning over her I whispered in her ear, "Justified." As I pulled the trigger and blew her brains out.

Breathing deeply feeling no regret and no remorse, I checked my watch and saw that I had an hour to shower, change, burn my clothes and get home to take my girls to where they needed to be.

All of my brothers started to pat me on the shoulder. I was thankful as fuck that I had them. They were the best of the fucking best.

Savage and Gage started the clean-up while I headed to the clubhouse and to my room to shower and change.

Walking in my front door it was to the smell of french toast and I moaned. "Please tell me you made extra?"

I smiled when I watched her put her hand on her hip and sneered at me, "What do you take me as? An idiot?"

Grinning, I walked forward, placed a kiss on Laci's temple. Then I did the same with Michelle.

Grabbing my plate I headed to the island, got a bite of french toast, and grinned.

It was as I was taking a bite I heard Michelle's inhaled breath.

Looking into her eyes it was to see that her attention was on my knuckles that were split open.

Looking for Laci it was to see she was eating her breakfast in the living room while she watched morning cartoons. I said in a low tone so she wouldn't hear, "Going to tell you something, don't want you to freak out. Need you to keep this shit to yourself, babe. Only ole' ladies are privy to this information."

"Okay?"

"Person who set your house on fire."

"Who?"

"Mina." Anger morphed on her beautiful face.

"I want a shot at her."

I was all in with this woman, smiling. I said, "Don't worry beautiful, she got led pipes to her knees, a hammer slammed into her vagina, and a bullet in her head."

I expected her to run, but no. She just sat there and then smiled, "Good."

Winking at her I said, "Revenge is always best served cold."

What she told me next shocked the fuck out of me, "Am I your ole' lady?"

"That's your question? Not how could you do something so morbid like that?"

"Cam, you're a biker in a motorcycle club. My daddy was a biker in the same club. No one fucks with you and yours. Now answer my question."

"You tell me, baby."

"I'll think about it." She tossed me a wink over her shoulder as she headed to get ready for work. Seeing that Laci was already dressed I finished eating then cleaned up the kitchen.

After dropping Laci off at school for her last day before summer break I drove Michelle to work, "Have a good day at work baby."

She paused when she was halfway out of the truck, "Cam, can you do me a huge favor?"

"Yeah, name it."

"I took your advice and signed up for the courses I need for my doctorate. You'll be there for Laci when I need you right?"

"Of course."

"Good. I have a course that takes place at another hospital for my doctorate. Mom is going on a cruise with her friends, can you watch Laci? Since it's summer there is no school."

I didn't need to think about it, "Yeah. I got her."

The moment that came out of my mouth, her entire face softened, "Thanks, Cam."

Grinning all the way to the garage at the clubhouse to get some builds finished, I walked into the clubhouse first. Luckily Powers wasn't busy, "Hey brother, got something to run by you, make sure it's cool."

"What's up?"

"I know we don't have anything major going on in two weeks. Michelle has to go out of town for some class she needs for her doctorate. Needs me to watch Laci."

"Yeah, that's good man. Let Lil know if we need to help out in any way."

"Appreciate it, man. You need me, I'm there."

"We got this. Take care of your girls." Smirking, he walked off.

Damn right they were my girls.

That night after dinner I stood in the doorway as Michelle packed her things. Laci sat on the bed and asked, "So I'm spending the week with Cam?"

The tone that she used with her daughter was something else entirely, she only spoke to her that way, "Yes baby, is that okay?"

Then I watched as a grin formed on Laci's face and a mischievous smile formed as well, "Totally. On one condition."

Shaking my head, just like her momma, I asked, "What's that peanut?"

"You gotta take me to the fair that's happening tomorrow." Tossing my head back I started laughing.

"Already planned on taking you there peanut. Also got a few things planned."

Her hazel eyes widened, in a soft whisper she asked, "Really?"

"Really." Color me surprised when she launched off the bed and threw her arms around my neck.

Bending into her, I wrapped my arms around her small body. This little girl already had me wrapped around her pinky finger.

The next day after we waved Michelle off I grinned down at Laci, "You ready?"

"Yes!" She ran to the truck with me laughing the entire way.

The moment we were both out of the truck, we walked hand in hand, paying for our tickets.

Standing there as Laci rode on one of the rides I felt a woman brush my shoulders, stepping to the side to move away from her, she did it again. How did I know it was a woman? Because the damn woman bathed in goddamn perfume.

"Hi. It's not often to see a man that looks like you at a county fair." Nodding, my eyes never left Laci.

The woman said huskily, "Cat got your tongue?"

"Watching my girl lady, spending the day with my girl." My eyes never left Laci.

I ignored the woman as she tried to make small talk. Thank fuck the ride had ended, this woman's perfume was giving me a headache.

The moment Laci reached me where I stood just at the entrance she said, "Cam. That was so much fun." I smiled down at her.

The moment she had her hand in mine I finally looked at the woman. "Do you mind?"

Seeing that she wasn't going to get anywhere with me, she finally moved the fuck out of my way.

"Who was that?"

"Some woman that doesn't know how to take a fu-freaking hint."

"Nice catch there." She giggled.

"Hey, brother." I nodded at Powers and then smiled down at Storm and Rosa. Laci hadn't gotten to meet his kids when we were at the clubhouse.

"Hi, I'm Rosa." Powers' daughter said to Laci.

"Hi, I'm Laci with an I," Laci said proudly.

"That's a cool name."

"So is Rosa." My girl and her manners.

"Do you want to go on that ride with me?"

She looked up at me and asked, "Is that okay Cam?"

"Yeah, peanut. I'll be right here watching."

"You got eyes on her like a fucking hawk brother." Powers said, I didn't have to comment, and neither did he for his daughter and son.

"Her mom trusted me with her. Eyes won't be looking anywhere else." And for the last two hours as she rode ride after ride, played game after game, not once did my eyes leave her.

"Have fun peanut?" I asked as I started the truck up.

"Yeah, Cam. Best day ever." Grinning, I drove us home.

Smiling when ten minutes into the drive she was curled up asleep with the big ass giant stuffed dog that I had won for her by pitching baseballs at milk bottles.

Lying in bed I kept inhaling Michelle's pillow. I was fucking addicted to her scent.

Jesus Christ, I was getting even deeper. Fucking A. I was ecstatic.

We were sitting on my, well our couch if I could get her to see it my way, while we watched a movie about two sisters that lived in the snow. Shit. This little girl better be lucky that I already love her.

However, forty-five minutes into the movie I was hooked. My man card was going to be revoked if anyone found out about this.

And here I sat singing along to *Let It Go* with Laci while Sparks, her crested gecko sat on her lap completely ignoring us. I didn't see how that was possible, even though our singing sounded great in my head, I could only imagine what we really sounded like.

But the moment the song was over and we stopped, fits of giggles came from beside me.

I had researched them the night that Laci had shown me Sparks in his tank. Shocked would be an understatement that Sparks tolerated her touch, even though she wasn't touching him but he was laying on her pajama bottoms.

The night as the ending credits rolled, I realized that Laci was dead to the world, softly snoring.

Luckily, when I picked Laci up to put her to bed, Sparks stayed still. He also allowed me to pick him up and put him in his tank. Thank fuck.

The next day while we were heading out of the house to go to the clubhouse for a cookout that Saturday, Laci had held something out for me, "What's that?"

"Something I made. Well, I made two of them. You don't have to wear them or anything." Her little voice shook with trepidation.

Kneeling down in front of her, I held out my hand and smiled when she placed two friendship bracelets in my hand. I saw the one that Laci and her mom had. Tears gathered in the corners of my eyes. Sniffing them back, I lifted up one and asked, "I'm honored peanut. Can you put it on my wrist?"

We had just walked in the clubhouse when Lincoln walked up to us bent and dropped a kiss on Laci's forehead, then his eyes landed on my newest addition.

"I'm hurt, darling girl. Where is mine?" Lincoln asked as he put his hand over his heart.

Then rocking my world, Laci spoke loud and for all to hear, "You won't be getting one because Cam is my person."

Smirking, I looked down at her, "You're my person too peanut."

Then in a whisper, she said, "You should've been my daddy."

I wanted so badly to tell her that if I could get Michelle to my way of thinking, first chance I would be seeing my lawyer and starting adoption paperwork.

Dropping to my knee, uncaring who saw and heard, I said, "Peanut, blood doesn't make a parent. Your mom gives me the go-ahead, I plan on making you my daughter in every way imaginable."

Tears gathered in her eyes, watching one fall down her cheek, I leaned forward and kissed it away. Softly she whispered, "Love you, Cam."

I poured my heart into four little words, "Love you too, peanut."

Later on that night I got a text from Michelle, they had to cut the course early due to bad weather moving in and she was on her way home. She asked me not to tell Laci, smiling, I told her we were at the clubhouse.

Lincoln had just broke out his guitar which caused Gage to grab his as well.

Around the fire pit as everyone settled in with moonshine and lemonades as they started to sing, *Kickin' It In Tennessee.*

Just as they started on the second chorus I felt someone's arms wrap around my neck.

My body tensed until I caught a whiff of that all too familiar perfume.

Smiling, I tilted my head to the side when Michelle placed a kiss on the side of my neck, "There's room baby."

With that, she rounded the chair, climbed on the opposite side of where Laci was sleeping. I had the two loves of my life laying their heads on my chest.

Realizing the magnitude of this moment I had just hit the highest point in my life, my world stopped spinning for me, and it started spinning for these two.

I'm trying to see things from your point of view,

but I can't stick my head that far up my butt.

Chapter 14

Michelle

Two weeks later I was on my shift in the hospital when there was a commotion at the double doors.

"Ms. O'Connell!" I whipped my head around to see Mackenzie as she was running beside a cop that had something wrapped in a blanket in his arms.

The moment I made it to the trauma room where the cop laid the bundle on the bed, my breath froze in my lungs, seeing the blue bow lips on the baby had me snapping out of it as I asked, "What have we got?"

"My baby. My baby." A woman came running into the hospital, just as a nurse was about to intercept the woman, two cops merged on the woman, maneuvered her to the ground, and read her Miranda rights.

Looking down at the baby it was to see the little white powder beneath her nose. Snarling, I said, "Everyone hands-off."

Grabbing gloves I grabbed a test kit, swabbed the powder, placed it in a vile and then I handed it to the officer.

With that done I nodded and we started to work on the baby.

An hour later when we got the answer to what the powder substance was we started the baby on a detox, a cocktail of drugs that the baby should have never had in her system. Who in their right fucking mind gives cocaine to a fucking baby?

Thankfully the baby got here in time before any more damage could be done.

Turning to Mackenzie who had blatantly defied another doctor's order to leave the little girl's side I said, "Call Child Protective Services." The thankful look she gave me wasn't lost on me.

This would keep her close to the baby's room until our social worker that worked solely with the hospital could get there.

Mackenzie stood there for a moment as she placed a kiss on two fingers then placed them on the baby's forehead as she turned and walked out of the room.

An hour later I heard my name being called as I was going over the little girl's test results, "Michelle."

Lifting my head to see the social worker, I nodded and offered her a kind smile which she returned, "Alice."

"We will do a DNA swab to see if the father is in the system. I hate to pray for it but this little one needs all the help she can get."

"What was found?" Mackenzie asked. It also helped that Alice was her aunt.

Normally they weren't supposed to share this kind of info with us, but the moment I saw Mackenzie when she had laid eyes on this baby, I knew that it was needed.

"Conditions that I hate to see. The little girl's name is Wren. She didn't have a crib to sleep in. She had a fucking cardboard box in the fucking hall closet." It took everything in me to not call Cam and have him break into the police department and kill the woman.

What I didn't know was that it would be taken care of, but not by Cam.

Two hours later after we did a DNA swab, Alice had returned with a file folder in her hand, "The father?" Mackenzie asked.

"Yes. We contacted him thirty minutes ago. He is on his way up here now."

I was praying that the father was better than the mother, "Some people don't deserve to be parents." I agreed with Mackenzie.

She had just stepped back into Wren's room to hang another IV bag when Alice approached the counter.

"Mr. James." Alice stepped forward as I looked up from my tablet where I had just entered a patient's information.

"Lincoln?" I stared at him as he looked up and the moment his eyes lit on me he sidestepped the social worker and then wrapped me in a hug.

"Lady told me you saved Wren's life. Thank you." Smiling, I patted his back.

The moment he let go, I pulled away and asked, "Wren? She's your daughter?"

"Yeah, that's what the bitch named her. But I do like it. It's different. Didn't even know about her. The chick, hell I don't even remember her damn name."

"Do I need to call Cam?" I asked.

"Nah, they're already on their way up here." I nodded.

"Mr. James, my name is Alice, we spoke on the phone." She offered him her hand as he shook it. "Ready to go meet your daughter?"

"Yeah." It was then that the brothers walked off the elevator. Seeing my man I winked at him then followed Lincoln and Alice to the room.

Just as I stepped in the room beside Lincoln it was to hear Mackenzie singing softly to baby Wren. No one moved nor said a word as we waited for Mackenzie to finish.

"Mackenzie?" I called out.

The moment she turned in her chair to take everyone in, her eyes landed on Lincoln and froze.

Smiling a small smile I made the introductions.

"Mackenzie, this is Lincoln James, Wren's father. Lincoln, this is Mackenzie, she's your daughter's nurse."

What was funny was that everyone had moved into the room except for Lincoln. No, his eyes were on Mackenzie.

"Mr…"

"Lincoln." He said huskily.

"Lincoln." She smiled shyly and I had to turn my face so she wouldn't see the grin on my face.

Seeing Lincoln shake his head moments later then walk to the bed where his daughter lay caused me to turn to Lil, June, and Melia, whispering softly I said, "I get off in an hour. Do y'all want to go get Wren some things?"

Each of them nodded softly. Since Laci was having a sleepover with my mother Cam and I had a free night. Sadly instead of remembering that I needed to refill my prescription for birth control, it totally slipped my mind.

And that was how I found myself with the women buying everything that Wren would need.

To say Lincoln was shocked when we arrived at his house pulling bags among bags out of our vehicles was an understatement.

When Cam and Heathen came out and grabbed the new furniture pieces then started to set them up in a room, causing Lincoln to hang his head and point, we all started to give Wren the life she should have had.

Love is composed of a single soul inhabiting two bodies

Chapter 15

Cam

Rousing awake from the dream I was having, everything in that moment slammed hard into me, that dream hadn't been a dream at all.

My woman's mouth was on my cock as she stroked it with her tongue. And then she wrapped her hand around the base of my cock as she started to move even faster with her mouth.

Wrapping my hand in her hair letting her know I was awake it only took a few seconds before all of my cum was bursting out of my cock into her mouth.

She swallowed everything down that I gave her.

***

My hands were shaking as I climbed out of the truck to help Michelle get Laci out of it and to grab the dishes that she had made.

"Pop-pop." Grinning, I held Laci's hand as we skipped up the front walk to Michelle's grandfather's house.

After I sat the dishes down on the counter I looked to her grandfather and said, "Mr. O'Connell, do you have a minute to speak to me privately." I asked as I fingered the ring in my jeans pocket.

He nodded, grabbed two beers, and then I followed him out to the back deck.

Handing me one, I took the cap off then took a swig of the beer.

"I already know what you're going to ask, the answer is yes. Laci told me what you did for her in her room without saying a word to either of them."

"I had a speech all prepared too." With a smoker's tone, he laughed.

"You fuck up again, I'll end you." I nodded in answer. I fuck this up again, I'll end my own self. I now realized that after she had been attacked, she had a wall around her heart. I hadn't even been close to the center of her.

Oh, but I was getting closer.

Swallowing down the emotions I nodded then offered the man my hand. The moment he shook it, Michelle's mother Anna stepped through the sliding doors, seeing that our conversation was finished, and said, "Dinner's ready."

The conversation flowed around the table as I was brought into the fold. Michelle knew about my parents; they were killed in a car accident the day after her father passed away from Pancreatic Cancer.

The next day we were at the clubhouse, looking at the double doors as they opened I saw a tiny slip of a woman as she walked in. She looked scared out of her mind. Stepping in right behind her was Walker. Walker was the Road Captain of our Clearwater Chapter.

"Hey man. What's up?" I asked him.

He had a look on his face that I had seen multiple times, "Powers and Lil here?"

Immediately, I softened my features, "Yeah, let me get them in his office."

Standing I walked out to the courtyard, seeing Powers I whistled. The moment I jerked my chin I nodded over to Lil.

They both made their way over to me, "Dove. Office."

He nodded as he grabbed Lil's hand and walked into the clubhouse. Upon seeing them, Walker led the woman to the office.

That woman caused fear to ripple through my body. How could a woman as stunning as her look so beaten down and defeated?

I Immediately calmed down when Michelle wrapped her arms around me from behind, leaning into her touch she asked, "You okay?"

"Yeah. A Dove just walked in here." I had sat Michelle down and explained to her what we did outside of the bike builds when I was going to be away from them for a few nights.

She had understood. The degrees to which she accepted everything about me were staggering, and I wasn't sure that it was really only because her father was a member that she was so well adjusted.

But then, her face softened and she proved once again why I fell head over heels in love with her, "Anything I can do, let me know."

A couple of hours later I looked over to see Lil holding onto the girl's hand, anger was written all over Lil's face and a murderous scowl was on Powers' face.

"When I get back, Church."

Nodding, I placed out a call to have everyone at the clubhouse. Clutch wouldn't be there because he was in the middle of a huge ass back piece.

Speaking of that I needed to go see him and add some ink to my tattoo.

Four hours later my hatred for what had been done to the woman, Cora, was growing with each thought that ran through my mind.

The hatred fled however the moment I parked my bike, walked into the house, and got a hot kiss from Michelle.

Sitting there cross-legged as I helped Laci wrap her mother's birthday presents, I was halted when she spoke, "Cam, can I ask you something?"

"Yeah, peanut?"

"Mom talked to me about things." She was biting her bottom lip. The same thing her mother did when she was nervous or scared.

"Things?" I asked.

"Yeah, about how I came to be."

"And how do you feel about that?"

"I'm not going to lie and say that it hurts. I think it hurts mom more than me. Sure, I would've liked to be made out of love, but mom has told me countless times that I was the reason she faced each new day with a smile on her face and why she didn't let that not saying the word that mom said, to beat her."

"Your mom is a strong woman peanut, and you're going to grow up and be just as strong. I can tell these things." I chuckled softly.

But there was something that was still weighing on her mind, how did I know that? I just knew it, "What else is there peanut?"

"I... I never wanted to ask mom what he looked like or who he was, I didn't want to cause her any more pain."

"Peanut, not going to tell you how I know what he looks like, I'll not mention the motherfuckers name. He doesn't deserve it. But let's just say that I don't see any of him in you. What I see in you is all your momma and the man above gave you my genes. Simple as that."

"I love you, Cam." Every single time those words come out of Laci's mouth I feel like I'm the luckiest son of a bitch in the world.

Staring into her hazel eyes that are so much like my own I said, "Love you too peanut with everything in me."

And just when I thought she had gotten out everything she wanted to say, she then said, "So…since the decision was taken from mom, on who my father is, do you think I should get the decision of who I chose to be my father?"

Unsure of where she was going with this line of questioning, I sat there as I thought about what she said, "Yeah peanut. Blood doesn't make a parent."

"Okay. Love you, Cam." I had two loves in my life, Michelle, and Laci.

Grinning, I said, "Love you too, peanut."

That was when she grabbed a manilla folder that was sitting on the coffee table. When she handed it to me I saw the look in her little hazel eyes. She was nervous.

The moment I opened the manilla folder I froze as I read the first line. *Application for Adoption.*

"You don't have to. I talked to mom about this." She was nervous, I didn't know why, but she didn't have to be.

Grinning, I reached for a pen that was sitting on the coffee table and signed my name. "As if I wouldn't sign this, I already consider you mine darlin'. The moment I laid eyes on you; it was a done deal. Hell, even my brothers already call you my girl."

After that was done, she shocked me with what she said next, "Dad, the man that raped mom, do you think that he will get what's coming to him?" She almost asked it so quietly that I wasn't sure if I heard her correctly.

"I know the man is burning in hell, peanut," I told her as I looked at her.

Laci looked up at me then, her eyes widened. She knew. She knew what I had done. Then she hurled her body into me, threw her arms around my neck, and cried.

Michelle came out of the kitchen at a run when she heard Laci crying, "What's wrong?"

I looked at her and mouthed, "She learned I killed that mother fucker."

Her face softened as she turned and headed back to the kitchen to finish dinner.

That night as I read her a bedtime story, just as I was about to read the next sentence, Laci asked, "Daddy, why do I look so much like you?"

I hadn't told Michelle this. But when I looked up before I answered her, it was to see Michele standing there in the open doorway, "Darlin' come in here. Something you both need to hear."

The look she gave as she walked into the room made my heart skip a beat.

"The reason why you look so much like me is that the man that raped your mother is really my half-brother. I didn't know any of that. Thought Porter was just our friend. It never even occurred to me; I knew that we look alike but still."

"It was Porter?" Michelle asked me.

"Yeah, baby. You did scratch his face up pretty good though." She had told me that she had blacked out and she didn't remember any of it, not until she was in the back of the ambulance.

"So I really do have your blood flowing through my veins?"

"That you do peanut. That you do." Laci amazed me, even more, each day.

You know when you're in love when You can't fall asleep,

because reality is finally better than your dreams.

Chapter 16

Michelle

Three days later walking into the clubhouse with Laci's hand in mine didn't cause shivers like it had been doing. Which was what caused me to smile wide.

A week ago, Cam had turned that bad spot in the compound's front yard into a more memorable spot. My vagina was waking right back up at those memories. God, I really was a hoe.

Cam had everyone stay inside the clubhouse while he fucked me deliciously on the side of his bike.

When we had walked into the clubhouse while I was wiping my lipstick from his lips, hoots and catcalls filled the night air. I placed my face on his shoulder and started to shake with laughter.

"Yeah. Damn proud to call you brother." Heathen chuckled from where he sat beside June.

Lincoln was sitting with baby Wren in his arms and I couldn't help the smile that broke out over my face. I seem to be doing that a lot lately, "That's the baby I was telling you about Laci."

Normally, I didn't tell her about my day nor the patients, but when she had asked why I had looked so sad I had told her that a baby had been brought into the hospital, the baby wouldn't stop crying so the mother thought to give her a bad drug. A very bad drug.

The moment we reached Lincoln and Wren, I smiled down at her. She was perfect.

And what did my daughter do? She placed a kiss on baby Wren's forehead then she caused not one dry eye in the clubhouse, "We aren't related, but in a way we are. I'll be your big sister."

"That reminds me," Cam said as he walked over to us.

The entire clubhouse quieted down when he reached us. I noticed he held two boxes in his hands.

"What is it?" I asked.

Then Cam dropped to one knee right there in the middle of the clubhouse in front of Laci and me.

"Michelle, I've loved you from the moment I laid eyes on you. I'm not going to say I'm sorry for that night, because had that not happened you wouldn't have had Laci and I wouldn't be this fucking happy to have a daughter. You're the air I breathe. You're the beat to my heart. I don't want to go another second without you and the entire fucking world to know how I feel. You accept me for me. Not once have you ever tried to change me. I'll be there when y'all are scared, to kill anything that dares to threaten y'all. I'll be there to wipe every tear Laci sheds and kick the little punk's ass that caused it. For all of that, all I ask is for you to say yes. Say yes to forever with me, and even beyond then."

That was when he handed one box to me and the other box to Laci.

I stood there as we all watched Laci open her box, then the thing tumbled to the floor as she threw her arms around his neck and squealed out, "Yes."

Inside the box was a property kutte and on the patch above the heart read, *Daddy's Princess*.

Smiling, down at them, I then opened my own box and saw my own property kutte, "Well mom? Give my daddy a yes."

"That's not all." He was still on one bended knee with Laci in his arms when he reached into his kutte pocket and pulled out a black velvet box.

Placing the box on the nearest table I opened the box and saw it. We had been in the back of his truck when we were teenagers and I happened to be scrolling on Pinterest when I saw the ring. The ring that was perfect for me. And there glaring me right in the face was that ring.

"Searched high and low for that ring."

"Well, what are you waiting for? Put it on me." I had tears trailing down my cheeks as Cam did just that.

I smiled when he wiped a tear away as he stood with Laci in his arms and then I threw my arms around the both of them.

We stood like that as I placed a scorching kiss on his lips.

After I let go of him, he placed Laci down on her feet then nodded to her kutte. "Let's get it on you peanut."

What I didn't know was that June had been taking pictures of everything. After he helped put my own kutte on, shots were poured and sparkling apple cider was placed in solo cups for the kids.

"To Cam, Michelle, and Laci. Thank God Cam got his head out of his ass. Cheers." Powers chuckled when Cam flipped him off.

It was strange to see that, you wouldn't expect the President of an MC to take that kind of insult lightly, however, the relationship that Powers had with these men was like nothing I have ever seen before.

I didn't know about any other MC's but what I did know was that none of them were like ours.

Later that night we celebrated our engagement and him making me his ole' lady officially, and suffice it to say, we both fell asleep without cleaning up.

***

Two Days Later

I had just got off the phone with the insurance company when Cam and Laci walked in the door with dinner.

"How'd it go?"

"Thankfully my insurance was up to date. They already received the police report and they're cutting the check."

"Yeah, that's great baby." He smiled as he placed a kiss on my forehead.

"I need to buy a new truck." Sadly, I had my truck in the garage that night when my house had been burned down.

"Yeah, we can go ahead and get you a new truck baby." Stubborn man.

"Cam..."

"Honey, that property kutte on your back and that ring on your finger means I take care of mine and you agreed to let me."

Knowing he wouldn't budge on this, I sighed and nodded, then I got a good idea, "One condition."

He eyed me curiously, "And that is?"

"You let me pay for a trip to Disney world."

He lowered his head and sighed. I knew that would work. Laci and I were his world and there was nothing that he wouldn't do for us.

I knew that fact to be true when he simply nodded a scant second later.

Love is a promise, love is a souvenir,

once given never forgotten, never let it disappear

Chapter 17

Cam

Three weeks later the moment we had our bags packed and out of that hotel and in the truck, I breathed a sigh of relief. The last week went like this.

"Daddy, let's go on that ride."

"Daddy, look at Minnie Mouse."

"Daddy, take a picture with me."

And did I argue? Nope. Seeing her smile and the numerous giggles that came from her were worth it.

"All that kid wanted was a chocolate freeze pop." *She had grumbled when a kid pouted and the dad told him no, that he had to wait for their complimentary dinner.*

So there I was, buying an extra chocolate freeze pop, handing it to Laci, and nodding over at the little boy.

As we stood there and watched as Laci handed the little boy the ice cream, Michelle wrapped her arm around my waist and whispered, "I love you, Cam."

I was about to lunge at the man when he sneered down at my girl who had a heart of gold, then I watched as

Laci tossed a smile my way and grinned. The man looked over at me, seeing my kutte, and stepped back from Laci and nodded.

Fucker was about to have his block knocked off.

Having the quietness in the cab of the truck, thank fuck. Disney World was fun, that was for sure, but goddamn was it fucking loud with kids screaming and squealing at everything that was in sight.

For the first time, I didn't have any music playing. And fifteen minutes into the drive back home, both of my girls had fallen asleep. With both of my girls wearing Minnie Mouse ears.

And when we pulled up at stoplights, did I bother to take off the Mickey Mouse ears, no, no I did not.

Three months later I was sitting with the brothers for my bachelor party. I hadn't wanted any strippers, Michelle would kill me, besides, I had the woman of my dreams, why would I want to look at naked women?

Just then I felt those all too familiar arms wrap around me from behind.

"You will not get drunk tonight. I want our pictures to look great."

"If I can't get drunk the night before our wedding, when can I get drunk?"

"After we say I do. After pictures. And after you pull me into a coat closet and make love to me with a wild passion."

So I did the only thing I could, "Yes ma'am."

She winked at me, bent at the waist, and whispered, "You won't regret it."

"Happy wife, happy life." So I downed my last beer for the night.

Grinning, she kissed me hard, my damn cock got hard. Fucking hell.

Turning my head to watch her walk out of the clubhouse with Lil, June, and Melia for her bachelorette party, my eyes were all for her ass. Whoever said a woman with curves was nasty, they needed to be hung on the tallest tree. By their dick.

"Goddamn, you lucky fucker." Lincoln smacked the back of my shoulder.

Yes, I was lucky indeed.

That night I stayed at the clubhouse, as ordered so I wouldn't see her the day of the wedding. I was on pins and needles.

I stood beside Powers with Savage, Heathen, and Greek as my best men, while we waited for the wedding to start.

She had asked us to be in light-washed jeans, a black button-up shirt with the sleeves rolled up to our forearms, and in our kuttes. Like she had to beg.

We had passed this field four weeks ago, on a ride with the club. Thankfully, Greek knew the owner and he was A-Okay with letting us get married in this field. His payment? Doing a memorial for his late wife on his gas tank.

I had tried to pay the man more because I didn't think that was fair and his words would stick with me for the rest of my life, "Boy, my woman would have been out here making sure the field would be perfect for your wedding, and if I didn't get out there with her, well I wouldn't be having supper that night. Not to mention she would've held her body from mine and there is nothing that I wouldn't do to make sure I had that whenever I wanted it."

"Are you ready for this brother?" Powers asked.

"Born ready."

When Melia started down the aisle with June following, and then Lil, my breath caught in my throat.

Seeing Michelle in a blood-red dress had my cock rock fucking hard. It hit just above her knees. Seeing her in that, Jesus Christ, the moment we said I do, I was finding somewhere to fuck my woman.

As they started to make their way down to me with her grandfather on one side and Laci on the other, tears hit my eyes.

I just couldn't wait anymore. I moved down the aisle, causing them to stop their forward motion, nodding at her grandfather, grabbed her hand and Laci's, and pulled them up the aisle. All the while our family laughed.

"Who gives this woman's hand in marriage?"

It wasn't her grandfather or her mother that said the approving words, no it was Laci, "I do."

Grinning, when Powers asked for the rings, Savage placed two of them in my hands.

First I knelt down in front of Laci, grabbed her right hand, and said, "Laci, I promise to always be there. To love you. To protect you. To play with barbie dolls. I promise to never tell you no for our princess tea parties. I promise to always let you paint my toenails bright fucking pink. But most of all I promise to be the best man that I can be, the one that God and your mother chose to be your daddy."

With that, I placed a miniature ring like the one I was placing on Michelle's finger but I placed it on her ring finger on her right hand. "As you get older, we can have it resized."

Kissing her cheek I stood, then grabbed Michelle's hand, "My heart. My life. My world. I promise to be there to get the lids off of jars. I promise to give you a foot massage every night because you are out saving lives and it's the least I can do. I promise to never forget an important date. But most of all, I promise to love you, to handle your heart that I have held since you were fifteen years old with the utmost care." With that, I placed her ring on her ring finger on her left hand.

Then with tears in her eyes, she grabbed my left hand and placed the ring on my finger, and nodded. She just fucking nodded? What the fuck?

Chuckling, I asked, "No words?"

"No, because you're a shit. You read my vows, memorized them, and stole them." I threw my head back and laughed. Yeah, I had done that.

We were in the backyard of the compound after she officially became my wife. Lantern lights lined the area. The brothers from the other chapters had shown up for the wedding and now, everyone was drinking and cutting loose.

We had already danced our first dance as husband and wife and I held Laci's hand in mine as we walked off the dance floor to our daddy-daughter dance when Cotton stepped up to me and held out a beer for me.

Nodding, I took it.

"Good God, she's the spitting image of you brother. Apple didn't fall far from the tree, that's for damn sure." Cotton nodded as he took Laci in.

This wasn't the first time that I had been told that, and never not once did I bother to correct anyone.

She was my daughter regardless.

"Actually he's not my dad biologically but he was built to be my dad." A lump formed in my throat each and every time she said that.

I couldn't be more proud of her even if she were of my blood.

Cotton looked at me and nodded, "Yeah, I get that darlin'."

"Time for pictures," June called out. "Michelle, Cam, Laci can y'all come over here please?"

Seeing that Michelle was already making her way over there after she handed Wren back to Lincoln, I grabbed Laci's hand as we headed in her direction.

June had a sign in her hands that she wasn't letting me see, looking at Michelle she had a blank look on her face so I shrugged.

"Now, Cam, will you please stand with your back to Michelle?" When I did that she placed Laci in front of us at our sides.

That was when she handed Laci a sign.

June wasn't holding the same camera as before; no, she was holding Laci's polaroid camera.

"Okay one two three." I heard the click.

The moment she was satisfied Laci sped off, hid the sign then came back to us.

Curious now, I took in our family's expressions and saw they were all smiling wide.

It was then that June held out the polaroid picture to me. Taking it, I looked at the sign that Laci was holding with a big smile on her face.

Coming soon to tear the world apart.

May 2022

Realizing what that meant I looked at Michelle and saw that she was smiling wide, "Surprise!"

Grinning, I dropped to my knees and placed a tender kiss on her belly. I was the happiest man alive and I couldn't wait to welcome our newest bundle to our family.

It is not that love is blind. It is that love sees with a painter's eye,

Finding the essence that renders all else in the background.
- Robert Brault

Epilogue

Cam

Standing beside Savage we both watched as Gage ran his hands through his hair while he was on the phone.

He was at his wit's end with Conleigh. He wanted to help her so badly but she wouldn't allow it. I knew that it was only a matter of time. Gage was a proud man, if Conleigh didn't realize what she had in him, it was going to be too late for her.

Looking over at my wife it was to see her walking over to me as she placed Cruz in my arms, "Please put him down for his nap?"

Nodding, I placed a kiss on her temple and tucked Cruz in the crook of my arm, "Is that a nap?"

"Yep." I grinned unrepentantly at Savage.

The only way Cruz slept was if he was in my arms. Sure it put a damper on our sex life but boy did we find times to fit it in.

Since the pregnancy with Michelle had been so horrible, the doctors had to take her reproductive organs.

Four months earlier

Sitting beside Michelle's hospital bed with Laci on my lap we ran a wet washcloth over her forehead. Her water had broken twenty-one hours ago. Her pregnancy with Laci had run so smoothly that we thought this pregnancy was going to go as fast as that one had.

We had been so wrong.

When Michelle started to get pale and the nurse checked the monitors that were beeping, she had slammed a button behind Michelle's head and then all hell broke loose. A nurse had asked us to step back.

"Their heart rates are dropping. We need to get them into the OR right now. Someone will come to get you when it's time to start."

Without arguing, knowing how important it was not to argue, we sat. And we sat. And we sat.

Three hours when no one had come out to get us I walked to the nurse's station with Laci's head laying on my shoulder, she was sound asleep.

My brothers had offered to take her but I couldn't seem to let her go.

"My wife. I was told someone would come to get me but..."

It was then that the double doors opened, the baby was in a clear plastic container being pushed out right in front of my wife.

Leaving the nurses station as I approached my son and my wife, "Mr. Bryant?"

"Yes." It was then that my brothers and their wives all stood and walked over to us.

"I'm sorry that no one could come and get you. The moment we started their heart rates dropped so we had to get the baby out. The sac that the baby was in had ripped which caused a rip in her uterus and she was bleeding internally. We tried several different extremes to stop the bleeding, the only thing we could do was to remove her reproductive organs. Your wife is now stable but she will be monitored for the next twenty-fours closely."

It took my wife eighteen hours to wake up. I refused to see my son until his mother could see him with me.

The moment I held him in my arms and handed him to my wife, all of the turmoil and devastation over the last two days had been wiped away.

And now here I stood with Cruz in my arms and Laci up on Lincoln's shoulder while his woman held Wren, we waited for the B's to be called.

The moment her name was called, "Michelle O'Connell Bryant," our entire group at the back of the auditorium cheered and whistled.

Did it bother us that everyone sitting there stared open-mouthed at us? No, it did not.

My heart was full as I watched my woman, my wife, my ole' lady walk across that stadium to accept her diploma. All in a navy-blue gown and cap with gold tassels hanging around her neck while she proudly wore her property kutte.

Two months later walking into the hospital to have lunch with Michelle, the moment I heard, "Dr. Bryant." I grinned like a cat that ate the canary.

"Oh Dr. Bryant, your husband has come to feed you." She looked over at me and grinned just as a child leaned over the bed and puked all over her legs.

***

Cam

Ten Years Later.

Walking into the clubhouse I had murder in my eyes as I walked over to March one of the prospects we had patched in five years ago and his son, Derek, with Cruz hot on my heels, we stormed over to them.

"Why did you tell my girl she was stupid?" I growled out.

And without waiting for Derek's response, Cruz brought his knee up and kneed Derek in the balls. "My sister isn't stupid. She's got more brains in her little pinky than you have in your entire body."

"I told her she was stupid because she wouldn't give me a chance."

"I don't blame her. You're not man enough for my big sister." With that Cruz walked off.

"You bother her again, your dad, brother or not, I'll kick your goddamn ass."

That night, Laci came over to us where we sat making s'mores, "Whatever y'all said to Derek, it worked, he hasn't looked at me once."

She grinned as I handed her the s'more I had just made.

And that was when another chapter of Wrath MC that Cotton had started years ago walked in. We all looked at the brothers walking in, but when I looked at Laci, I gritted my teeth.

She had a look on her face that I had seen when Michelle looked at me.

I had another ass to kick. Onyx. The Icer for our Georgia chapter.

The End.

To find out more about Cora, please make sure you are subscribed to my newsletter to receive her free book. Wrath Ink.

If you subscribe and you don't receive the book please message me on Facebook.

The link for both is on the next page. Thank you!!

Connect With Me

My Website

Home - Author Tiffany Casper (mailchimpsites.com)

Facebook

https://www.facebook.com/authortiffanycasper

Instagram

https://www.instagram.com/authortiffanycasper/

Goodreads

https://www.goodreads.com/author/show/19027352.Tiffany_Casper

Other Works

Wrath MC

Mountain of Clearwater

Clearwater's Savior

Clearwater's Hope

Clearwater's Fire

Clearwater's Miracle

Clearwater's Treasure

Clearwater's Luck

Clearwater's Redemption

Christmas in Clearwater (December 2021)

Dogwood's Treasure

Dove's Life

Phoenix's Plight

Raven's Climb

Falcon's Rise (September 2021)

Wren's Salvation (October 2021)

Lark's Precious (November 2021)

Sparrow's Grace (January 2022)

Crow's Forever (February 2022)

Warm Hearts (TBD)

DeLuca Empire

The Devil & The Siren

The Cleaner & The Princess (TBD)

Novella's

Wrath Ink (Free with subscribing to my newsletter)

Hotter Than Sin

Standalone

Silver Treasure

Printed in Great Britain
by Amazon